MURDER ON THE CALEDONIAN QUEEN

Helen & Martha Cozy Mystery

SIGRID VANSANDT

 Created with Vellum

For my daughter, Kate. All my love always.

Chapter One

Martha Littleword lounged on a well-worn tartan blanket, drowsily looking up into a perfect blue summer sky. She'd taken a free day from her typical work schedule and scampered off on a meandering walk down to the bank of the River Calder. Having already eaten her lunch and snacked on one blueberry donut, Martha lay blissfully pondering whether to have the second donut still tucked in her knapsack.

Down the sloping hillside and forty-feet below, two lazy narrowboats drifted by almost noiselessly. The engines' gentle chugging sound, a heartbeat for the entire summer landscape, harmonized with the chortling and merry conversation of the many birds busily taking care of their young families and daily housekeeping.

Martha shut her eyes with a sigh of gratitude at Mother Nature's fathomless beauty. At the caresses of the gentle August breeze, dipping and playing across the field, her sock-free toes would occasionally wiggle happily like nubby, white blades of grass enjoying the heat of the afternoon sun.

"I think it's time for tea and that donut," she murmured, a faint smile spreading across her mouth.

A shotgun's ear-splitting explosion, firing over where she lay, froze Martha's entire body into a rigid, stunned human plank. All of her limbs, including the once happy toes, froze as if instinctively knowing that movement was a treasonous act against life itself. A second blast followed the first.

It was her brain, egged on by a Marthaesque vehement distaste for injustice and crimes against peacefully resting donut consumers, that riled her finally into action.

"What the heck!" she screamed at the top of her lungs. "SOMEONE is lying over here!"

She swiftly rolled over onto her belly and raised her head ever so turtle-like above the foot-tall grass. Off in the distance and higher up the knoll, a curly-headed blonde woman, dressed in tweeds stood shouldering a hunting gun. From where she lay hidden like an offended and unfairly hunted game bird, Martha saw the woman was walking away. Another person, a man, joined the huntress and pointed toward a copse of trees. Who were these interlopers on Healy's grounds? With their guns safely quiet, Martha wanted to know, so she jumped into a full bipedal stance and waved her arms.

"HE-E-Y! YOU UP THERE! D-O-O-N'T SH-O-O-T!" she yelled with all her might.

The man and woman turned a regal stare in Martha's direction. Looking down on her from their elevated position much the same way two Greek gods might curiously study a lesser life form, the modern-day Apollo and Artemis, each returned Martha's frenzied salutation with a cool, half-hearted wave from their one weapon-free hand.

Seeing and sensing a chilly aloofness in their demeanor, a tinder of irritation smoldered in Martha's craw. The earlier Eden quality of the place with its peaceful kinship among the species was lost. Two brutes had come in and wrecked it for everybody else.

Hastily slipping on her tennis shoes, Martha started her climb up the hillside. With each step, she wondered who the people were and what they were up to. Though they must have seen her hurrying toward them, they turned their backs and walked away.

"Hey! Hey! One minute, please!" she called trying to arrest their departure. "I want to ask you a question!"

As she watched, she saw them give a slight shrug and sigh, probably preferring she stay down in the grass and accept her fate as either a bird-of-the-field or a common grey rabbit.

"Warm, friendly types, I guess," Martha muttered but pushed forward. "Kind who like to shoot guns. A good thing to remember, Martha," she panted to herself, her lungs burning.

Within twenty feet of her quarry, she stopped. Better to suck in some air and not appear too out of breath. Her quick assessment of the pair made her glad she was at least attempting to act in shape. Noting the man and woman were both fit, well dressed in expensive hunting togs, and looking like models from the glossy magazine, *Gun & Game*, Martha mentally congratulated herself on her own unique, albeit eccentric fashion sense.

Today she was wearing her ripped-up sweatshirt with an undershirt she'd gathered from her bedroom floor. Both were showing signs of the soup she'd dribbled from lunch plus a smattering of golden cat hairs from Gus, her cat. Her jeans were vintage Levi 501's which, in her opinion, looked amazing even though they were from 1985 and had a patch on the butt that read "Bam!".

Fully oxygenated, Martha pushed further up the hill and forced a smile, "Hello. I was down below, there," she pointed to where her old blanket was lying. "My name is Martha Littleword and I live in Marsden-Lacy. I don't think we've met before."

She offered her hand first to the woman who took it and returned the greeting.

"I'm Coraliss Redfern and this is my husband, Reny. Do you realize you're on private land?"

The tone was blatantly snobbish and hostile.

Reny Redfern made no effort to offer his hand, so Martha dropped hers. She brushed her red hair away from her face, and as she did so, her hand caught against a piece of grass lodged there. Realizing she must look like a wild-woman from the moors, she internally chastised herself for not staying hunkered down and undiscoverable in her spot below.

Surely, she thought, she was still on the Healy estate, not someone else's. She'd walked no more than a mile or two that morning. Her course had been meandering, but not without direction. Perhaps, these two were some of the guests or experts for the Antique and Art Festival her two dear friends, Helen and Piers Cousins, the owners of Healy, were holding to aid the Marsden-Lacy Animal Shelter. Martha came at Coraliss and Reny from a fresh angle.

"Yes, I am aware this is *Piers and Helen Cousins'* property. I work with Helen. She's my partner."

Martha waited for their response. Though slow in coming with marked expressions of uncertainty, the gun-laden couple shrugged and appeared to accept Martha's credentials.

Reny reached over proffering his hand to Martha which she took.

"I'm here to give a lecture on medieval map making," he said. "I've known Piers for quite some time. We studied at university together."

Martha mentally subtracted the woman's age from the man's. At least a twenty-year difference between husband and wife.

"Nice to meet you, both," Martha said. "It will be a fun event. Are you staying at Healy House?"

This time Coraliss responded.

"Yes, though Reny is doing a lecture, it's more of a hobby. We're friends of the Cousins, *not* the regular experts or staff from some auction house or museum."

"Staff?" Martha echoed.

"Yes, you know, the staff coming to assess the value of items brought in by the public."

Martha heard the bite in her new acquaintance's tone. It was clear; Coraliss wanted to make sure she was counted among the elite, not the working rabble. The earlier smoldering tinder of irritation caught and turned into a nice blaze in Martha's heart. It was time to needle Mrs. 'Upitty' Redfern a bit.

"Of course, of course. It's a mistake anyone could make. Even I, at first, thought you were Piers' gamekeepers, but they're rarely armed with such big guns, so I thought you were town folk up for some illegal poaching."

Martha offered her best snobby-person laugh.

Neither of the Redferns responded, but Martha knew the comment hit its mark.

"We're heading back to the house," the younger of the two Redferns snapped, her slim mouth melting and curving into a feline-like smile. "Hope you enjoy your *tramping* about the countryside."

"I will, thank you," Martha returned without showing she was interested in Coraliss' verbal slap. "Until the shot-across-my bow earlier, I wasn't aware there was hunting on Healy's grounds. What are you bringing to dinner tonight?"

"I hardly think we are out trying to bag dinner," Coraliss snipped.

Reny shrugged and explained.

"We haven't taken anything today. Only sighting in our guns. In a few days, however, we intend to take advantage of the Glorius Twelfth in Scotland. If you're not familiar with the sport, it's the day grouse season begins. They're great flyers, you see. Fast, very fast. Piers is going with us after the antique and art fundraiser."

"Helen cannot come," Coraliss pointed out. "She's busy working or *something*."

Martha was tired of pretending to be pleasant. They were boring, plus they intended to kill defenseless wild birds for fun. She wondered why Piers or Helen would be interested in either of them. Time to cut this conversation off at its ankles.

"I'm sure it *is* something, all right. Well, it's been fun and potentially lethal running into you both, but I've got to get back to eating a donut on my tatty blanket down by the river. Try to keep your aim above my head, if you would."

Martha, flashing an overly animated grin, turned and left the pair with a hearty wave and a 'Ta!'.

"Poor Helen," she grumbled once she was sure there was enough distance between herself and the Redferns. "Bet she's glad she's not off to Scotland with that pair. What kind of person shoots innocent birds for sport?"

No sooner had the words left her lips than another round of gunshots blasted overhead causing her to jump, stumble and land squarely on her back end.

"Well, I'll give you that, Coraliss Redfern. You certainly got the last word."

Chapter Two

St. Columba's Monastery
Island of Iona, Scotland
July 24, 825 AD

The morning was cold and the boy, Aidan, huddled in his woolen robe out of the wind. He chose this hiding spot to be within view of the church, but high enough upon the rocky outcrop that he was invisible to anyone below. A Viking longship, anchored off the edge of the island, bobbed and swayed with the seas' relentless waves. Within minutes, the cruel, greed-driven men onboard would come ashore. Terrified and alone, the taste of copper filled Aidan's mouth.

In the church below, he knew the eleven remaining monks, including their abbot, Father Blathmac, were prostrate on the stone floor waiting for what would be a brutal death. If the wind were not so strong, he might have heard the men's fervent prayers for their souls. The thought of the only family he'd ever known being slaughtered was too horrible for Aidan's young mind to comprehend, so he prayed for the Northmen to spare them. Their chances were grim. Already the Vikings had burned and plundered many of the monasteries in the Northern Isles of Ireland and Scotland. Few monks survived, and those that did, the Vikings took away in chains to become slaves.

Father Blathmac, Iona Abbey's seventy-five-year-old abbot, had come to this center of the Celtic Christian religion a year ago. He was well aware of the Viking threat to undefended religious settlements, especially when the Vikings believed the monasteries were repositories of gold or silver encrusted relics. The pagan Northmen wanted not only the wealth but the divine power they believed to be imbued in the sacred items. Death was certain if you refused the Vikings their booty and Abbot Blathmac had come to Iona deliberately to do so. His intention was martyrdom.

He gave all of his monks the option of leaving that morning. A few had gone, but some also stayed. Those that went, were probably already down the hidden pathway on the other side of the island and pushing off in a small currach, or boat, made of wood, ox hides, and tar. They would sail for Ireland and live to tell their story. The men below would not.

When the Northmen's boat arrived, Aidan had been allowed to leave, but he wanted to stay. Father Blathmac had been kind to him. Teaching him to read and even making sure he had proper clothing to wear. He loved the old man like a real father. Blathmac agreed he could remain on the condition he stay hidden and serve the abbey, even if the Northmen destroyed everyone and everything.

It would be a difficult job for the twelve-year-old. He was to wait and watch. Father Blathmac gave him instructions. If the Vikings burned the church and started digging up the grounds in search of the holy relics and manuscripts, he, Aidan, must watch to see if they unearthed the hidden relics.

If the Northmen found what they'd traveled hundreds of watery miles for and took from Iona the illuminated manuscript made by St. Columba along with his holy bones, Aidan was to take a currach and follow the monks who'd returned to Ireland and confirm the sacrilege. Christendom had lost more brave souls and two of its most treasured relics to the pagans.

Crouched behind a massive boulder, his heart beating hard in his young chest as the raiders disembarked from their boat and within mere minutes invaded the stone and wood church. Aidan heard the cries of the monks being slain. He covered his ears and steeled himself to not run. Fear and shock caused his body to tremble, but soon there was only the sound of the wind and the chattering of the seabirds overhead.

After a short time, the raiders came outside and set fire to the church. He saw they carried nothing other than their weapons. Their leader, a mid-sized man powerfully built, took his bloodied sword and indicated to his men to search the area. With the church in flames, great billowing clouds of black smoke rose high in the air. Aidan thought of the monks out in the sea on their currach. They would see the smoke and know their beloved home and brothers were gone.

As the day turned to afternoon, Aidan watched the Vikings tire of digging in random spots. They loaded on their back what food they found and returned to their longboat. The single sail rose and within an hour, the ship disappeared around the headland along the northern coast of Iona.

Gingerly, Aidan picked his way among the rock-strewn hillside until he was on flatter ground near the tiny settlement. He headed straight for the church, now a shell of blackened rock. Once there, he peeked through the doorway, seeing the charred remains of the monks scattered about the floor. One body lay at the altar, Abbot Blathmac's. The boy made the sign of the cross and knelt at the door, offering a prayer for his dead. He would come back and bury them, but first, he must fulfill his promise.

The monks many centuries before his time had excavated and worked an area of land to create an underground series of domed cells constructed by rock. Using dirt and turf, they cleverly covered and concealed these from view. A hidden aperture opened into a descending tunnel where a man crawling on his hands and knees would, within a few yards, reach an internal domed space normally used for private prayer by the monks. Today it was the refuge for the Ionian relics.

Since the inception of the Viking raids, the monks had worked at concealing this particular subterranean cell. Protecting the heart of Iona, the holy bones of St. Columba, was their priority after following their founder's discipline of monastic life. It was nearly impossible to find the cell's opening. Again, Aidan scanned the horizon and the sea for either ship or man. Certain he was alone, he walked away from the church toward a built-up terraced area for growing vegetables. The Vikings had stripped the garden of all its produce, but in the middle of the place was a simple stone Celtic cross only a foot tall resting on another larger square piece of rock. The monks had duped the raiders. As the Vikings gleaned the vegetables, they missed the real treasure only six feet below their grasping hands.

Making another sign of the cross because this was a holy space he was about to enter, Aidan pushed the stone cross to its side. It moved easily, revealing the passageway below. Climbing down quickly, he traversed the tunnel and came into a chamber. At the center, a hand-sized clay lamp burned, allowing Aidan to see his surroundings.

Like sad, displaced children, the remaining illuminated manuscript not taken by the fleeing monks, the gold and silver covered cask with the saint's holy bones inside, and many other valuable liturgical items along with two sacks of food sat in the middle of the hallowed room where the monks only hours ago had hurriedly placed them. All was as it should be.

Aidan climbed the tunnel again, leaving the valuable items to wait for the monk's return, and relaid the stone Celtic cross.

It took him many days to bury his dead. Once done, he packed some remaining food into a satchel and followed the path down to where another currach waited in a cave near the sea's edge.

Weeks later, Aidan would make it to the abbey at Kells just inland from the northeastern coast of Ireland. He told the story of the Northmen's butchery, the burning of the church, and how Father Blathmac refused to hand over the illuminated manuscripts and St. Columba's holy bones.

In time, the Christians declared Blathmac a martyr and a saint. His act of courage as the Vikings tore his limbs from his body so bewildered and impressed the Vikings, many would later convert to Christianity. The Northmen never forgot Iona or Blathmac's act of certainty in his god.

For the next twelve centuries, the precious illuminated manuscript made by St. Columba's hand would be the desire of kings, diplomats, religious crusaders, and corporate businessmen. All would play a part in its final fate.

Chapter Three

Saturday
Healy House, Yorkshire

"Gerta, I agree it is quite an...*extensive* collection but unless you have some copies from before 1905, they don't have a substantial monetary value," Helen Ryes was saying, "but they do have aesthetic, educational and personal value."

Her tone was kind, empathetic, and patient, but Gerta Grisholm, a buxom woman with metallic blue eye shadow, was undeterred in her quest for monetary justification.

"My nephew's girlfriend works in a used bookstore in Leeds. She says I can sell these online and make a fortune. What about that, Mrs. Ryes?"

Gerta's demeanor was defensive and pugnacious.

"Give it a try. You never know what the market will bear," Helen, her feet tired from standing and her stomach hungry, was ready for lunch.

Healy House's Antique and Art Appraisal Event was going wonderfully. It was late afternoon and Helen's line of curious, hopeful bibliophiles, all carrying boxes of books, magazines, and even the odd framed manuscript page, stretched another five people deep behind Gerta.

With a huff, Gerta picked up her box.

"I don't know why I paid the entrance fee if all you have to tell me is my mum's collection is worthless."

Her voice carried down the line to the others waiting patiently.

"I don't believe it *is* worthless," Helen stated, her tone chilly. "If you would like, I will give you the name of a gentleman in London who is building an extensive archive of magazines. He has a massive warehouse, and your collection may interest him. It would depend on what he already has from this publisher. I wouldn't want you to go away feeling underserved, Mrs. Grisholm."

Out of the corner of her eye, Helen saw Martha standing under a food tent and munching on a corn dog.

"Do you want one?" her friend mouthed and pointed at the deep-fried, delicious, but bad-for-you, cornmeal wrapped hot dog.

Helen's stomach rumbled in the affirmative, and she gave Martha a discreet nod.

Quickly scribbling the London address on a piece of paper and handing it to Gerta, Helen hoped this peace offering would mollify the fussy woman. Out of the corner of her eye, she saw Martha making her way toward her with the corn dog.

"I don't feel this has been helpful," Gerta quibbled, her voice rising with a hint of the eager attention seeker. "I'd like the name of an actual expert."

Helen's mouth compressed into a flat line. Her inner temperature climbed. It was already warm enough in August under the tent and the last thing she needed was to have a hot flash. Quickly perusing the faces of the people in her line, she saw the mixed expressions of annoyance and uncertainty.

As she opened her mouth to say something, she heard Martha's voice behind her.

"Hey Gerta," Martha said, her voice low as if she was trying to be tactful, "I saw two teenage boys using your car for a park bench.

They were having a mustard-packet fight. Not good for the old paint finish, ya know."

"Did you tell them to get off? Really! Well, if you ask me, this event is being poorly managed," Gerta bellowed. "Shouldn't security be in the car park protecting people's cars from vandals?"

Gerta's voice carried across the front lawn, making heads turn to see who was causing such a furor.

Helen and Martha exchanged glances.

"It looked like your daughter and her boyfriend were monitoring *things*...from the backseat," Martha answered.

Gerta's face turned red, and her mouth puckered up into a sphincter-like protuberance. Sucking in some air, she let it out again with an exacerbated, "That is a lie, Martha Littleword!"

"Don't believe me, go look."

Gerta turned with military precision and marched off in the car park's direction resembling with every step, an affronted, puffed-up pigeon.

The next man in line stepped forward and placed a book by Ernest Hemingway on the cotton tablecloth in front of Helen. He was a man of late sixties and middle height. His white hair stood out around his head like a halo. From his expression, it was clear he was excited to hear Helen's appraisal.

An Art Deco-styled Greek figure under a leafless tree decorated the book's jacket cover. It was Ernest Hemingway's, *The Sun Also Rises,* and with great care Helen opened the front cover, running her finger down the title page.

"Hello, Mrs. Ryes," the man said. "I brought this today for my wife who doesn't like crowds. The book was her aunt's who lived in Paris after World War One. It's signed by the author. Thought it might be worth paying the entrance fee to find out if it had any value."

Gently turning the pages, Helen didn't speak for a long minute. She looked up at the man with a bright smile.

"You have an exceptionally valuable book, sir."

Martha signaled to the security personnel standing by the tent's opening to come forward.

Helen continued.

"Have you had it appraised before?"

The man grinned and with joy explained.

"No, but my brother-in-law has been sniffing about my wife's bookshelf and I saw his face when he saw this book. He's a dodgy duffer, so I wondered if it might be worth something."

Helen laughed.

"It would be good to have another appraiser also look this over for confirmation, but this is a 1926 first edition. Charles Scribner's Sons in New York was the publisher. It has the misprint on page 181. The book is well-loved to be sure. The binding is creased, and there is some mildew within and some foxing issues. Nothing a good conservator couldn't stabilize and repair. I would put its value at between ten and twelve thousand. If you get the signature validated, it will be worth much more."

The man clasped his right hand to his chest and exclaimed, "I'm gobsmacked! You for sure it...it's worth that?"

An excited group huddled around the table, and more people were crowding closer.

"I didn't catch your name, sir?" she asked.

He rattled his head back and forth, an expression of happy bewilderment on his face.

"J.D. Greer."

"Mr. Greer, I believe the book is worth a considerable amount of money. It would be wise to have it properly valued and insured. If your wife decides to sell the book, she should meet with one of the major auction houses or reputable book dealers in London. They will counsel her and procure the best price for the book."

Mr. Greer looked stunned. He ran his hands through his white hair.

"I'll be honest with you, Mrs. Ryes. I don't feel comfortable taking this book back home. Anything could happen. What should I do?"

"You should call your bank and if you have a safe deposit box, it would be a good idea to put it there until your wife makes her decision."

Helen turned to the security officer standing beside her and said, "Please take Mr. Greer home, Henry. If he drove his car, better follow him to make sure he makes it safely."

The officer agreed and the crowd slowly dispersed, leaving Helen and Martha with only a few people and items left to appraise. A man approached wearing a beautifully tailored suit and pulling behind him a suitcase on wheels.

"Hello ladies and gentlemen," he said. "My name is Daniel Kime and I will take over for the rest of the afternoon's appraisals."

"Thank you, Daniel," Helen said and excused herself.

She and Martha walked away from the tent arm in arm like old friends.

"Where's that corn dog you got for me? I'm starved!"

"Might be cold, but here it is."

Martha pulled the corn dog out of her tote bag and handed it to Helen, who took a voracious bite. After she swallowed, she asked, "After this is over, what do you think about going to Scotland for a week?"

"Not if we are palling around with those friends of yours I met yesterday."

"What friends?" Helen asked.

Martha shot Helen a smile. In her best silly Groucho Marx-like voice, she said, "He likes medieval maps and blondes with enormous guns. She enjoys rubbing elbows with money and shooting all things defenseless."

Helen nearly choked, her mouth full of cornbread and hotdog. Once she swallowed, she clapped Martha on the shoulder and laughed.

"You're so bad!"

"Call it as I see it, Helen."

"I think you met Coraliss and Reny Redfern, but we are most

definitely not going with them. That's poor Piers' weight to shoulder. *We* are meeting a young art advisor, Sasha Pelletier. She wants us to look at a rare two-volume sixteenth-century historiography by Holinshed called the *Chronicles of England, Scotland, and Ireland.* It was recently found in a church library. Sasha's client wants two more opinions before he buys it."

"Sounds exciting," Martha said. "When do we leave?"

"We need to be there next Saturday. Sasha wants us to travel up the Caledonian Canal on a hotel barge with her. We'll go inland by private car to see the document. It's under lock and key in a private home near Invergarry, Scotland. Sasha's client is picking up the tab. Does it sound fun?"

Martha squealed with delight.

"I'm already packed. I can't wait!"

Helen laughed.

"Good! It's settled. Scotland, here we come!"

Chapter Four

Dunadd, Argyll
Capital of Dál Riata
The new kingdom of Scotland
849 AD

Newly anointed King of the Picts, Kenneth MacAlpin, stood looking over the Moine Mhor, an expanse of bog that carpeted the southern end of Kilmartin Glen in the land of Argyll. He watched as a sizable contingency of his troops, followed by a small group of monks, headed toward his hill fort and family seat, Dunadd.

They'd retrieved two of the relics of St. Columba. The saint's gilded bones and a famous manuscript from Iona were in MacAlpin's keeping. The timing was perfect. Report of a massive fleet of Vikings sailing down the northwestern coast reached MacAlpin only the previous evening. He wondered if the remaining Ionian monks would leave in time for the abbey in Ireland.

The removal of the relics had been difficult for the ecclesiastical community. After the raid and death of Abbot Blathmac, the monks returned and spent twenty years laboring to rebuild the church. Being a small group, the task was arduous and because of the never-ending assaults by the Norsemen, the Columban monks spent more time in Ireland than on Iona.

Iona's days of being a religious powerhouse were ending and MacAlpin knew the northwestern islands were impossible to protect from the Scandinavian raiders who controlled most of the northern lands. It was a matter of time before the Vikings finally found the holiest of all the relics; the saint's bones and the illuminated manuscript. Keeping the most important holy items in Celtic Christendom in an indefensible place was no longer tenable.

MacAlpin, the first ruler of both Pictland and Dál Riata, the kingdoms were later known as Scotland, had an ulterior reason for removing the spiritual core of Iona. After subduing the Pictish chieftains through war, MacAlpin needed to consolidate his power and justify his kingship. He needed a new heart, something powerful to bind the two kingdoms into one. St. Columba was the key.

The troops and monks were coming through the fort's first entrance. He was curious to see the relics. St. Columba's gilded bones were over two-hundred and fifty years old, and the monks considered the manuscript as the most beautiful creation by human hands in all the world. MacAlpin had few pleasures in life. This would be one of them.

With haste, he went to meet MacDonald, his first in command.

"Have the monks bring in the casket and I will talk first with the abbot."

"One of my rangers brought word there is a fleet of Norsemen on the move in this direction," MacDonald said. "They've entered the River Add at Crinan and mean to take Dunadd."

"We will see the holy relics, first. Bring the abbot to me."

A man of forty years with sad, intelligent eyes came into the hall. He wore a belted tunic, leather shoes, and his head was bare. MacAlpin accepted the offered blessing and pointed to a stool. The two men sat down together.

"You are welcome here, Father," MacAlpin said. "I would offer you and your brothers food but not accommodations. You will travel on tonight to Dunkeld. I will follow after we put down the Norse threat."

The abbot nodded.

"You have our prayers and our gratitude."

"I need something more," MacAlpin said. "I want you to confer a blessing on me today in front of my troops and my kinsmen. As St. Columba's priest, you will give *his* blessing on my throne."

The abbot's expression never flinched or showed a sense of surprise. He said, "I will bless you but I have no authority to sanctify your throne."

MacAlpin lowered his voice so only the priest could hear.

"I have culled together two kingdoms, neither wishing to be subservient to the other. The Vikings breathe down our neck on every border. Your monasteries have bled and will continue to do so. We need one king, one kingdom and one church. Today, on the ramparts, you will take Columba's relics, read from the manuscript, and sanctify my reign. Christianity will be the official faith of the Picts."

The priest swallowed hard and nodded.

"On what authority will I do this?"

"Mine," MacAlpin said. "And the authority I invest in you as my Bishop of the cathedral at Dunkeld."

Later, that same day, the new Bishop of Dunkeld in a ceremony attended by chieftains, monks, and soldiers, blessed the reign of Kenneth MacAlpin as the King of all Pictland.

MacAlpin's fame would grow, and history would declare him Scotland's first king. His cathedral at Dunkeld, at least for a while, was the holy center and heart of this new, proud nation. But if anyone should doubt his divine right to rule, they need only visit his cathedral.

For beneath the chancel steps rested the holy bones of St. Columba and adorning the altar shined an illuminated manuscript so magnificent, so venerated, some claimed, it was the work of Heaven's angels.

Chapter Five

Tuesday Morning
Highlands, Scotland

The Redferns stood on an outcropping looking across one of the many lochs dotting the Highlands of Scotland. Dressed for hiking, they'd already covered three miles up to a vantage point allowing them to see across the valley.

The day was clear. No clouds to obstruct their view as it stretched out for miles across the glen. Below them, majestic pines grew from the bottom of a deep ravine. On their way to the hunting lodge, they'd argued and Reny suggested they take a walk to clear their heads.

They didn't speak. Coraliss sighed.

"Reny, they'll investigate if it comes out."

"*If* it comes out," he replied. "And if it does, I'll have already moved on to greener pastures."

His wife turned to face him, her expression strained and worried.

"How can it not come out? You and father are fools, Reny!" she cried. "I read the reports from the engineers. You're putting thousands of people's lives in danger. If those planes fall from the sky, there will be a federal investigation. You'll take down the company, the investors, and my father."

Reny Redfern was glacially calm. He chuckled and went over to his wife.

"Why did you read the reports?" he asked, watching her with curiosity.

She shrugged his attention off and walked to the edge of the cliff.

"It was in the emails Daddy for some stupid reason cc'd me. I think he gets our addresses confused sometimes. It was an attention grabber, though. The engineer who wrote the report practically pleaded for an extension of time to work out the bugs."

"He was trying to extend the tests, dear," Reny said, "and also his funding. If you give in to project managers and their concerns, business would never get off the ground."

His pun made him chuckle.

Coraliss slowly turned to face him again. She wore an expression of disbelief.

"He said the software was untested in the air and he would not be held accountable for its failure. The man's wording was 'a catastrophe of horrific proportions may ensue'. You've got to stop the project from going forward."

"You don't understand, do you Coraliss? If those planes have an issue with their software, it won't matter. I'm selling my interests to Piers Cousins. We will leave him holding the bag."

"He's not a fool. How you coerced my father, I'll never know, but I saw how deeply involved he is. I read your emails," Coraliss rebutted.

"Your father, with a lot of my money filling up his re-election campaign funds, pushed through the certification to the aviation association. As for Cousins, he's only interest is diversification of his company's portfolio. Buyer beware is my motto."

"Reny!" she yelled. "I can't stand aside and not say something. You've got to do the right thing! People's lives depend on it."

Coraliss spun away from her husband to face the view once again, her blonde curls caught by the wind and streaming along her face. "I'll talk to my father. I'll stop both of you!"

Reny sighed. His eyes moved across open terrain, the loch below, and the hills beside where they stood.

"Well," he said, walking again to her side, his tone congenial and compliant, "I'll see what I can do. Normally, I never back-peddle in business, but your position is so..."

With a gentle hand to her back, he pushed her over the precipice and leaned over casually to see where she hit three hundred feet below.

"Final. Your position is final, Coraliss. I've taken every measure to clear things up."

Reny Redfern walked away from the cliff's edge with his business profits and future interests intact. A true corporate monster at the top of his game.

Chapter Six

St. Andrews, Scotland
10 April 1559

John Stewart, the fourth Earl of Atholl, and illegitimate son of King James V of Scotland, and half brother to Mary Queen of Scots sat in a pillowed chair drumming his fingers. He was comfortably residing at the priory house as was his right as the Commendator, Lord and inherited owner, of St. Andrews.

Times were tough, and money was short even with his income from St. Andrews. Stewart may be noble-born, but he was an illegitimate bastard whose purse never kept up with his lifestyle. Like in any age, most men, if they wanted to have power and wealth, needed to be self-made and start at the bottom, usually being kicked around for a while by those at the top.

But orbiting other political players wasn't for John Stewart. At twenty-eight years old, he wanted nothing short of total sovereignty over Scotland. Luckily for him, the Protestant Reformation was well underway, and it was flinging up opportunity all over the place like dung from a stable boy's pitchfork.

As his fingers continued to tap the table's wooden surface, a brilliant plan was forming in his cool, calculating mind. If King Henry IIIV kicked out the Catholics for money and power, why not him? The priory of St. Andrews was his by inheritance, and its income was substantial. What if he threw his support behind John Knox, the Presbyterian rebel demanding 'the boot' to all Popery?

As one of the leaders of the newly formed Lords of the Congregation, a group of five earls who'd pledged their lives to secure Scotland for the Protestants, Stewart was in an excellent situation to encourage the overthrow of Catholicism and secure its inherent wealth.

If they kicked out the ecclesiastical communities, there would be even more revenue. Stewart wasn't a fool. He'd seen how the wave of friary and church purges were taking hold across the country. People were making money hand over fist.

If he wanted to keep the valuables, the gold and silver from his appropriated priory for himself, he needed everything removed post-haste and installed at Castle Kincardine, the Stewart family ancestral home.

Though he was willing to toss away his religion for power, he wasn't comfortable destroying his family's patrimony. The holy, invaluable items entrusted to his lineage, he must preserve. It was critical to send someone tonight to Dunkeld to retrieve the precious bones of St. Columba and the illuminated manuscript on the altar.

A loud knock at Stewart's door brought him back to the present.

"Who is it?" he called.

"Your steward, my Lord," came the reply.

"Come in!"

The door swung open to reveal a tall, blonde-haired man of about thirty-five years of age. Wet from head to toe, William Keith had arrived minutes before from Kincardine Castle west of

Dundee. He was the right man for the job. Powerfully built and a military ranger, his family had served the earls of Atholl for three generations. Stewart trusted him completely.

"Shut the door, Keith," Stewart said, his voice low. "Come and set. Did you bring the men I asked you to?"

William Keith nodded.

"I have my Lord."

"I will have food prepared for you. Tomorrow you go to Dunkeld."

The steward did not ask why. It was for his master to tell him when he was ready. John Stewart considered his words before continuing. Removing the relics, should they still be in their rightful places, would be tricky. The chaplain of Dunkeld would know Stewart was a confirmed Protestant. The rightful recipients of the items should be the magistrates of the city, but Stewart wanted to leverage his hereditary right as the Earl of Atholl and the historical protectors of Dunkeld Cathedral. He would take the money and lesser valuables from the church as he was doing at St. Andrews, but at Dunkeld, he would do what was right by his kin.

"Tonight, two of your men will take those trunks," he pointed to three massive wooden crates sitting next to the wall filled with the booty from St. Andrew's, "to Kincardine and inter them under lock and key in the strongroom. *You* will go to the cathedral at Dunkeld and request the relics of St. Columba and an illuminated manuscript adorning the altar. The Saint's relics are under the chancel steps. See they are uncovered and secured in a wooden trunk with my seal upon the lock."

Stewart handed a leather satchel to Keith containing the letter to the chaplain, a lock, and a seal.

"Along with the abbot, you will send one of your three men remaining to you, to Ireland and the Abbey of Kells with the trunk containing the relics. Bring the manuscript wrapped in dry leather to Kincardine and store it in the strongroom until you have word from me. Do you understand?"

He took from his table a leather pouch filled with coins and handed it to Keith.

"Give this to the abbot for his journey. He is to send a return letter notarized by the abbot of Kells saying they have received the relics of St. Columba. After you and your men have eaten, prepare the carts and supplies, and leave. Time is of the essence. A revolution is coming. You are dismissed."

William Keith did part of what he was told. Removing the bones of St. Columba from Dunkeld, he saw to it they were transferred to the safety of Ireland, but in the process and along the way, he lost or buried the illuminated manuscript somewhere between Dunkeld and Ireland.

John Stewart had little time to worry about the lost manuscript. He was busy building his power base and manipulating others on his way to the top. It was all for nothing. In ten years, they would assassinate him.

The thing made of animal hides, vegetable dyes, metals from the Earth, and men's creative minds had been tossed about for over seven hundred years on the waves of ambition, intolerance, and greed.

Wherever it lay, secreted in its dark, forgotten tomb, the fates would surely play their hands and let it surface once more to test the souls of men.

Chapter Seven

Tuesday Morning
The Highlands, Scotland

Tucked back like a small bird in among the pine trees, Lucy McCreedie was fixing her binoculars on a Crested Tit foraging about the bark of a tall Scots Pine some fifty feet to her left. The weather was perfect, and visibility across the loch was crystal clear.

An avid bird watcher, she came up early to find a sequestered spot in hopes of glimpsing the delicate black and white bird. Dressed in colors to blend with the natural surroundings, Lucy was virtually invisible to friend or foe.

A soft rustling sound fixed her attention upward into the tree canopy. Her first sight of the nimble feathered bird poking about among the pine branches for its breakfast rewarded her immensely for the early morning trek up the hill.

Awe and joy spread across Lucy's face as she saw the precious, tiny creature with its recognizable crest atop its head come into view. He gazed down at her and cocked his head in greeting. The two species held eye contact for a moment until the bird took wing once more.

Sitting back, Lucy turned to face the landscape stretching out in front of her. A feeling of peace and wonder filled her soul. Across the way, two hikers stepped out and stood on a long cliff edge. Lifting the binoculars, she honed in on them.

It happened in slow motion, as she watched through the lenses. One hiker, a man, pushed the other over the cliff.

"What?" she half breathed, half groaned. "Oh my God!"

The binoculars dropped from her grasp, only the string around her neck keeping the glasses from toppling down the hillside. Grabbing them again and lifting them to her eyes, her hands shaking, she narrowed in on the cliff. The man was leaning over the edge talking to himself. He straightened up, and for a second, she saw his face as distinctly as she knew her own. With a calmness about his bearing, he turned and walked away.

Lowering the binoculars this time, her heart, like one of her beautiful birds, beat wildly in her chest and throat.

"I must have imagined it. Maybe there was only the man standing there."

She shook her head and looked back at the cliff. Fear gripped her. The place was so secluded. She'd not met anyone on her hike up to this spot.

"No, no," she repeated softly to herself. "I saw it. He pushed the person. He pushed them off the cliff."

Huddled with her back securely pressed against the Scots Pine, she kept still like an animal who's only safety was in not moving. With her mind firing options for getting back to her car and avoiding whoever was out there pushing people off cliff edges, Lucy tried to take slow, calming breaths.

Above her, birds were calling to one another in loud, sharp cawing and screeching sounds. She froze. A predator was coming, and the birds knew it.

Lucy pulled her knees up to her chest and tried to think. The sounds of footfalls came along the path ridge. Was it him? She tried frantically to assess if she was visible to anyone looking down over the hillside and if the huge pine's trunk hid her body completely.

"Please, please, God," she internally prayed. "Don't let him see me. Please."

She kept her head securely pressed against the tops of her knees, listening with the intensity of a mouse for the slithering of a snake.

The man's footsteps closed in, echoing down to her. Directly above the place where she was hiding, he came to a dead stop. As if on cue, all the birds in the tree canopy took flight at once. The rush of wings made Lucy almost scream out. An uncontrollable trembling took hold of her entire body. Holding her breath, she hugged her knees harder, waiting and willing the man to walk on.

"Go!" she commanded in her mind. "GO! Walk on!"

Like a blessing from above, he did as she demanded. His footsteps moved on and soon all was silent in the forest. She dared not release her fierce grasp on her aching, bundled legs. A sense of horror at what she'd seen twisted into a feeling of nausea.

With deliberate slowness, she opened her eyes. Perched not five feet in front of her was the Crested Tit bird. It cocked its head, first on one side and then the other. Unafraid, it hopped closer toward her feet, as if to assure her the danger had passed and she wasn't without friends.

An unsure smile quivered at the edges of Lucy's mouth. She released the pressure on her legs.

"He's gone?" she whispered hopefully to her tiny companion.

The answer arrived with two more of the ethereal, winged beings. Three Crested Tits flicked and fluttered about the pine forest floor within her reach, comfortable with her presence.

It took two more hours before Lucy stretched her legs and scrambled up the side of the hill to the path. With care and constant vigilance, she worked her way back to her car and practically flung herself inside the vehicle with grateful relief.

That afternoon, three park rangers and Lucy McCreedie found

the body of a woman. Interviewed by the police, Lucy told her story. She tried to describe the man's face she'd seen, but only remember the color of his blue jacket and dark hair. Unfortunately, the body had no identification and none of the other visitors to the park had seen a man hiking alone that morning.

The authorities issued a statement to the public asking people to come forward with information regarding the death of a young blonde who fell from a cliff under suspicious circumstances.

Lucy left her information with the police. Returning home to Edinburgh, she was accompanied by a ghost and a man's face forever etched in her memory.

Chapter Eight

Thursday Evening
Marsden Lacy, Yorkshire

It was an exquisite summer evening for a drive in the convertible. Martha's Mini Cooper, she called The Green Bean, hugged each curve of the road as if it and the blacktop were old friends. The huge topaz colored moon floated serenely above the purple Yorkshire hills while the sweet scent of cut hay perfumed the warm air.

The perfect old rock n roll song about the girl who wanted more fueled Martha's driving. She was on her way to Healy House to pick up Helen. They were meeting Sasha, the young art advisor from London, for a briefing at The Traveller's before the trip to Scotland.

With the fundraiser finished and Piers on his hunting trip, it was a good night to eat-out in Marsden-Lacey. The Traveller's Inn was hosting an Irish band and it was the peak of tourist season. The joint would be hopping.

Turning in through Healy's gates, Martha reduced her speed to a pleasant canter. Above her head, the ancient English Oaks lining the gravel lane hummed with the chortles and calls of night birds. A few dozen crickets nestled in their hedgerow homes added a back chorus to the evening's gossipy hubbub.

Healy House was a kiss for the eyes. Framed by hills with two stately yew trees flanking its corners, Helen and Piers' lovely old Elizabethan house emerged as Martha drove free of the oak-lined drive. She pulled the Mini into the curved driveway and stopped at the front stone porch.

"I saw you coming," Helen called with a happy wave as she swung down the stone steps. "It's so good to be out tonight. The last week has been exhausting."

In Helen's back-draft, Tidwell, Healy's butler, fussily followed to open his mistress' car door.

"How are you tonight, Tidwell?" Martha asked smiling. "I want to come back and stay for another weekend in the fall. I enjoyed your help with the proper usage of cutlery at the table."

Martha was grateful. Tidwell had taken her under his tutelage during her stay at Healy for Easter. Being the perfect English butler, his demeanor diplomatic and reserved, he answered, "Thank you, Mrs. Littleword, I am fine. I look forward to seeing you soon."

"Tidwell," Helen said, turning to him before getting in the vehicle, "please don't wait up tonight. I'll be late. Leave the garage area lit. I'll find my way without trouble."

With Helen ensconced and belted in the car, Martha put the Mini in gear and slowly drove it away from where the butler stood.

"You deserve a break," Martha said to Helen. "With all the hard work you've been putting in as Lady of the Manor, charity gigs, and managing our clients, a night-on-the-town is what you need."

As she watched Tidwell in her rearview mirror, an impish grin tickled the corner of Martha's lips.

"Let's see what Tiddy does if we crank the music real loud," she said.

"Oh good grief," Helen answered. "You've got it in your head Tidwell is your father. You love him and you love to tease him more."

"Maybe so, but there's always something about his reaction. He never fails to surprise. It's a game we play."

Martha turned the music back up, causing one of the stoic butler's eyebrows to raise. She revved the engine, inciting a definite pursing of his lips. As the car shot down the road, spewing a few pieces of gravel, Martha kept one eye on her rearview mirror. Tidwell looked surreptitiously around and preceded to moonwalk backward through Healy's front door.

Martha burst out laughing.

"Did you see him?" she exclaimed. "He moonwalked, Helen! I saw him do it!"

Helen's head swiveled to the rear to see.

"He did not," she declared. "Tidwell is the definition of..."

"A dang good dancer," Martha finished.

"A butler who can even dance," Helen sighed, her tone betraying a sense of fatigue.

Martha gave her a pat on the arm.

"How are things going? I can hear the tiredness in your voice."

Helen was quiet for a few seconds and shrugged her shoulders.

"Piers is so good to me, Martha. The staff is exceptional in every way, but I didn't realize how absorbed my life would be by his. I'm running every which way trying to take care of our work and keep up with *his* life. The Redferns were a nightmare."

"When did they leave?" Martha asked.

"Last Sunday and Piers left yesterday ago. He wanted me to go to Scotland with him. Honestly, I need some downtime."

She looked over at Martha, and her pretty smile was there again.

"Some girl-time, too."

Wrapping her arm around her friend, she squeezed Martha.

"I've missed you, too," Martha laughed. "It's been important that you've had time to get used to this new life, Helen. With me staying on top of our accounting and correspondence, I've been barely treading water. This trip to Scotland is what the doctor order for us both."

They were silent. The quiet, nighttime landscape unfolded in front of them.

"You, know," Martha said. "I got the feeling when I talked with Piers yesterday, he didn't want to go to Scotland. There was a definite hesitation in his voice."

"Piers and Reny met in college. Redfern was an executive for a software company and retired a few years ago from a high-level finance position. I think he's involved in something to do with the airline industry," Helen explained.

"He was pleasant enough," Martha said, trying to be upbeat for her friend. "Was Piers upset you couldn't go?"

"I don't shoot for sport, Martha. I never would. Even Piers didn't want to go, but…"

Helen's flow of words stopped. Martha knew to give Helen some time to form exactly what she was thinking.

"It's strange, but I don't like Reny Redfern and to be honest, I feel like I let my husband down because I didn't go with him."

Not a time to rush into a quick-fix response. Helen deserved a thoughtful one. Martha studied the road ahead as both women fell quiet for a few moments. Even though she was looking forward to having a fun girl week, her best friend's happiness came first.

"I tell you what," Martha said. "We will be in Scotland, anyway. Why don't we drop by the hunting lodge and give Piers and the Redferns a treat?"

Helen snorted and laughed.

"You hate hunting. The place will be filled with sad, moldy deer and stuffed boars."

"Now, Helen, is that any way to talk about Piers' friends?"

The night rang out with some hearty laughter, a few good nose snorts, and the life-affirming back-beat of a rock song about friends and the road ahead.

Chapter Nine

Thursday Evening

"Nice out!" Alistair Turner exclaimed, clapping Detective Chief Inspector Merriam Johns on the shoulder. "A double bullseye! You've been sneaking around on us, Johns. Did you hang a board up in your office?"

"Hey, hey, you two," Johnny O'Grady, the chief's darts partner, joined in, "that throw was pure talent. The man has a steady hand, he does. We're gonna win that tourney in Edinburgh Saturday. I bet my life on it."

The men laughed and took turns either shaking Johns' hand or congratulating him on his darts. Perigrine Clark, Merriam Johns, Alistair Turner, and Johnny O'Grady were playing a heated match while The Traveller's Inn was slowly filling up for a busy night. There was to be an Irish band coming, and the fiddler was first class.

"I think we're ready for the tournament, lads," Perigrine said, lifting his glass filled with a dark Porter to the other three.

"To taking the cup at Edinburgh, cheers!" Alistair said, raising his glass, too.

"Cheers!" Johns and O'Grady joined in to seal the toast.

"I'd like to take in some fishing while I'm up there," Johns added as the four men found a table near the back of the room. "It would be crazy to not take advantage of the season."

"Ten years ago, I was in Inverness for a meeting," Perigrine added, signaling to the barkeeper to bring another round, "and I caught an eighteen kilo Pike."

If anyone but Perigrine had made the statement, there would have been serious ribbing about his big fish tale. Since he did everything with panache, there were only appreciative head nods all around the table.

"You better come and go with me, Clark," Johns said. "I'd like nothing better than to reel in one that big."

The men chatted on about fish, darts, and the best places to eat while they were in Edinburgh, when out of the corner of his eye, Johns saw Helen and Martha walk into the pub. His face broke into a smile, causing the other three to turn about and see what made the normally stoic man show so much tooth.

"Back in a minute, chaps," he said and lifted himself from his chair.

He saw Martha and Helen moving through the busy throng of pub patrons. Martha's red, wavy hair was up in its usual ponytail and she was wearing jeans with heeled-wedge sandals. Another smile creased his weathered, handsome face. Though Helen's beauty was delicate and spoke of London's Bond Street elegance, Johns only had eyes for Martha. Her curves and youthful prettiness, even though she was well into mid-life, made Johns overly conscious of the competition he was up against.

"Hey!" he called out over the din of jovial human conversation. "Martha!"

Her head turned as her eyes scanned the room. Catching on his upheld hand over the multitudes, she gave him a sunny smile. He waved his hand, beckoning her to come to him. Nodding, she leaned over and said something to Helen.

His anticipation at seeing her lifted his pulse. They headed toward him, but a man intercepted them.

"That son-of..." Johns growled under his breath as he recognized Piers Cousin's Head of Security, Adam Buchanan.

The Irish band kicked off with its first lively song.

The crowd realigned their focus from the bar to the corner stage and pressed forward, stymying Johns' progress. Toes were tapping, one old man was jigging, as the fiddler ripped into *The Irish Rover.* In the music's uprush, Johns lost his bead on Martha, but he saw the tall Buchanan easily.

Adam Buchanan left nothing to the imagination in advertising his muscular physique. Tonight, he was wearing a tight black t-shirt with his military tattoo highlighting his beefy outer left bicep. Johns' irritation rose.

For the last three months, Buchanan had made no bones about his intentions regarding Martha. He'd even told Johns to 'push off' once during a community meeting after Johns asked to set down by Martha. If it hadn't been that Johns was the key speaker on de-escalating aggression in tough situations, he'd probably have punched him right there. From that point on, the tension between the two men escalated, even though Martha had made it pointedly clear she wasn't comfortable with Adam's attention.

The music in the pub gathered steam as did Johns' jealousy at the idea that Adam was pushing himself on Martha once more. Moving slowly through the clapping patrons, he saw Buchanan lean in, resting his hand against the wall. From the man's posture, Johns knew he had someone cornered under his overgrown arm.

He couldn't see if it was Martha, especially with such a bull-ox in the way. As the music climaxed and the entire audience was stomping the ground or singing along with the chorus, Johns saw Buchanan make his move. He pushed harder through the congested crowd.

As he reached for the muscle-man's shirt, a tapping on his back stopped him. Spinning around, he saw Helen smiling sweetly up at him.

"Hi!" she yelled. "We were trying to get through, but..."

Registering a confused, tense expression, he jerked his head around. But Buchanan disappeared as well as whoever it was he was talking to. *The Irish Rover* ended with uproarious applause.

"I've lost Martha," Helen said once the noise level dropped to a low roar. "Do you have a place to set?"

Feeling torn between the desire to find Martha or help Helen find a seat, Johns' brain and common sense grabbed the reins. He took Helen's arm gently, offered her a warm smile, and led her back to where his dart mates were sitting.

"Mrs. Cousins," Alistair said, standing up and offering her his seat. "So lovely to see you. Are you out enjoying the music tonight?"

As Helen sat down in Alistair's care, Johns slipped away to go find Martha once again. Seeing her coming from the ladies' room, he made a beeline in her direction. Feeling bruised and still warm with anger at what he thought he'd seen, he took her by the elbow leading her outside.

"What's gotten into you?" Martha asked.

"What's gotten into me is that overgrown ape, Buchanan. Every time I turn around, he's trying to schmooze you. Was that you under his puffed-up excuse for an arm?"

They had made it outside and were standing on the patio overlooking the canal.

Martha's mouthed dropped open and slammed shut again. From the snapping and glint in her eyes, he knew she was about to explode with indignation.

Instead, he watched her face morph instantly from fierce rebuttal mode to a slow cauterization of her inner anger.

She took a slow breath and let it out.

"I don't know what you're talking about, dear, but if you'll take two steps back and quit acting like a wounded bull, we can discuss whatever you're upset about."

Her eyes were wide with the look of a woman waiting for an explanation and it better be an excellent one. He stood up straight and took two steps back as she'd requested. Watching her face for signs of truth-fudging, he considered his next question carefully.

"Did Buchanan have you cornered? I thought I saw you talking to him."

"I *was* talking to him. He *had* me rather corned. As always, I'm polite to Adam. He is Piers and Helen's security head. If you're asking if I like his attention, I will tell you again what I've told you before—I don't enjoy it, but I'm quite able to take care of things myself."

"I'm gonna kill him," Johns grumbled and turned to go back inside.

Martha initially didn't follow but stayed rooted to the ground like a frozen, shocked statue, her expression conveying utter disbelief. But as Johns, like a stung stallion, covered the space between where they'd been and the pub's door, she jolted free from her immobile trance.

"Merriam!" she called to his retreating figure. "Do not go in there! I mean it! DON'T GO IN THERE!"

He spun around right as he reached the door and looked at her. She shook her head at him with slow deliberation.

"If you go in there," she shook her head again, "I don't want to see you anymore. I'm tired of this."

"He knows we are," he pointed back and forth between the two of them, "a thing! But he keeps pushing himself on you, making me look like a putz."

"If you go in there," Martha said coming closer to him, her gaze hard on his face, "and start something with him, Merriam, he might..."

She stopped speaking as if she wasn't sure how to say what she meant.

"What?" he pushed. "He will WHAT, Martha?"

"He knows Krav Maga. He told me he could kill men with his bare hands. He might...hurt you."

Her last two words launched an invisible flamed-tipped javelin of anger lodging itself into the part of his brain housing the male ego.

"Like Hell, he will!" he practically roared.

Turning on her and pushing through the door, he walked inside. The place was in full swing of another humorous Irish song called *Lanigan's Ball* about a party, mislaid jealousy, and the hullabaloo that ensues when men get sideways over a woman. Johns spied Buchanan facing the bar, drinking from his glass.

Plowing through the crowd, he came up behind Buchanan and tapped him forcefully on the shoulder. As Buchanan turned around, Johns gave him an exaggerated grin, swung back, and fired his right fist straight into Buchanan's jaw.

The entire place exploded. Buchanan had gleefully returned Johns' punch, which the young toughs in the bar took as an open invitation to whip themselves up into a full-out, fun-filled bar brawl.

The music, people yelling, and chairs crashing about crescendoed into a wild symphony of human insanity. Undisturbed by the uproar and the fight, the Irish band continued to perform a perfect high-spirited musical soundtrack to the brouhaha going on in front of them.

Perigrine, Alistair, O'Grady, and the publican, with expertise known to men in these situations, finally pulled the two instigators apart whereupon the place fell quiet.

Johns brushed off their restraints. Feeling pleased with himself for getting in more good licks than Buchanan, he walked out the pub's door just as a young, well-dressed woman walked in.

Chapter Ten

Thursday Evening
Marsden-Lacey

The pub's patrons turned and stared at the new arrival. Her face warmed with a blush at their concerted attention.

"Umm, is there a Helen Ryes Cousins here by chance?" she asked.

A few people shook their heads as others moved back to tables and chairs. The band picked up again, playing a sad song about a lost sailor while the publican, along with O'Grady's help, lifted Buchanan off the floor.

Helen came forward, offering her hand to the woman.

"You must be Sasha," Helen said. "I'm Helen. You've come in at, well, an unusual moment for The Traveller's. Please follow me. I have a booth in the back by the garden windows."

The two women found the table and settled themselves. Janie, the waitress, took their order. Out of the corner of Helen's eye and through the window directly behind where Sasha sat, Helen saw Martha's face lean ever so slowly into view.

Helen maintained complete mastery of her facial expression and continued to chat with her important client as Martha acted a short rendition of 'The Embarrassed Mime Who Wanted to Come In Out of The Garden'. She'd been hiding there since Johns' outrageous row with Buchanan.

Martha carried on for a few seconds through the windowpane with much finger-pointing and angry silent word mouthing, one sentence easily decipherable as 'Merriam is a jerk'.

As Sasha continued to explain to Helen about her client, she looked away to pull something from her satchel. Taking advantage of the moment, Helen did her silent rendition of 'Get Your Mime's Butt In Here!'

Martha's head sunk below the window seal with only the top of her red ponytail visible and flicking about like a squirrel's tail. Helen flashed Sasha a brilliant smile as the girl returned her attention away from her satchel and back to their conversation.

"I'm excited to work with you, Mrs. Cousins," Sasha was saying. "My mentor, Sir Alec Barstow, from Cambridge, recommended I meet with you. He enjoyed working with you on the Shakespeare folios you brought to auction. This should be another unique opportunity for your firm."

The red ponytail moved left out of the lower windowpane, disappearing completely to Helen's relief.

"As an art advisor to my client, I need two opinions on this rare manuscript. Sir Alec will be coming to Scotland as well," Sasha said.

"Sir Alec?" Helen exclaimed a genuine joy in her voice at the thought of seeing her old friend. "I adore that man."

"He's addictive," Sasha gushed. "I hated leaving Cambridge. I couldn't imagine not hearing his lectures anymore. It's a great honor to work alongside him. If we assure my client the Holinshed is legitimate, I expect to meet with him in London by the end of the month."

Sasha looked over Helen's head, indicating someone was coming down the short hall behind her.

"Hello," Martha's voice said. "I apologize for being late."

Helen turned around and smiled at her friend.

"Sasha, please let me introduce my colleague, Martha Littleword. Martha, this is Sasha Pelletier, our client."

The two women shook hands, and Martha took a seat.

"I was about to tell Helen," Sasha explained, "how excited I am to take advantage of the hotel barge experience. Departure is at ten o'clock this Saturday morning at Banavie. Once near Invergarry, we will travel by car to meet with Mr. Arthur McMurray, a bibliophile in his own right."

"Is he the current owner of the manuscript?" Martha asked.

"Yes."

"Will you be leaving to go up tomorrow to Banavie?" Helen asked. "Would you like us to follow you?"

"Actually, I'm staying in Carlisle tonight. My half-sister lives there with her husband and two children. I haven't seen her in three months and it's a chance to catch up."

Sasha packed her things back into the satchel.

"Here are your boarding passes for The Caledonian Queen. It should be a lovely way to see the Highlands."

"Thank you, Sasha, and we look forward to seeing you there," Helen said.

Everyone rose and they walked out to the car park. As Sasha drove away, Helen asked, "What happened between you and Merriam?"

Martha breathed deeply and let it out like a woman practicing yoga. She turned and faced Helen with an expression of serene indifference.

"It took every scrap of dignity I could muster in the garden," she thumbed over her shoulder in its direction, "to walk in the pub after his shocking behavior. I hope people don't think I had anything to do with it."

Martha pressed her mouth into a hard line.

"People will believe what they want to believe," Helen said. "It took real gumption to walk in here. If it's any consolation, you were the picture of relaxed professionalism with Sasha."

Walking toward Martha's Green Bean, they both sighed.

"Come on, let's go back to your house," Helen said. "I want a cup of tea and five of your homemade oatmeal cookies. It'll make you feel better, too, and honestly, I'd like to curl up in your guest room and just be Helen again for the night."

Martha followed her friend.

"That's fine, but you'll have to sleep with Gus. He's taken over the guest room bed."

"Okay. Is he going to be fussy because I'm sleeping there?"

"No, maybe a bit peavy at first, but he's a good cuddler once he realizes you're in for the night. He likes being tickled to sleep. Just don't let him be a bed hog."

"Typical man," Helen said, opening her car door. "It's all about him."

"Well, he *is* a cat, but he's a tomcat. Lots of his kittens are littering the neighborhood. Kind of territorial," Martha said, shaking her head. "Males! Maybe I should get him fixed."

Helen asked with a little laugh, "Do you mean Merriam?"

"Wouldn't hurt," Martha grumbled as she opened her car door. "You know what? Let's not think anymore about him tonight. Let's go home, make a pot of chamomile tea, get lots of blankets and pillows on the couch, and eat too many cookies. We'll watch an old mystery on tv and thank God for the women in our lives."

Helen laughed.

"You had me at too many cookies. Let's go."

Chapter Eleven

Friday
Balmore Lodge, Scotland

"Do you have one more cabin available? Excellent! Yes, if departure isn't until three o'clock tomorrow, we can make it. The name for the single cabin is Reny Redfern. Thank you."

Piers Cousins was on the phone with the cruise reservation company. He had tired of hunting by the second day with Reny. Since they'd met on Wednesday evening, there had been a distinct feeling of heavy pressure to commit as an investor in Redfern's software company.

This sense of urgency on Reny's part to get a signature from Piers raised red flags, and Piers back-pedaled creating a reaction in Redfern he'd never seen before. As they'd sat in front of the open fire one evening discussing the investment, Piers explained he would decide on the investment once he'd read over all the documents his team was assembling for him.

"Business and friendship, as you know Reny, is never a good

mix. I have to answer to a board, anyway. You'll have my decision after it has gone through the proper procedures and examinations."

In an instantaneous flash, Piers saw something predatory in Redfern's eyes, usually well-camouflaged by people at this level of business. From that point on, Piers was wary of him.

Later that evening, the topic shifted to a more congenial place. They discussed Helen's work and who she'd be assisting in Scotland. Redfern's entire demeanor changed. The idea of traveling up The Caledonian Canal by hotel barge and meeting the art advisor from London thrilled him.

"This Sasha Pelletier who's working with Helen, you say she's an art advisor? The name is familiar to me. I believe she's done some work for Coraliss and a new business partner of hers."

"Really?" Piers responded with interest. "I forgot how interested in antique maps and old manuscripts you are. Helen and Ms. Pelletier are meeting a man who claims to have a Holinshed but don't let on I've told you. Helen would have my hide if I let out information about her work. She's uncompromising regarding confidentiality."

Reny waved his hand.

"I'm a vault," he said, "but I'd enjoy seeing the Caledonian system. Let's see if they've booked all their cabins on The Queen. I have some business to clean up and I can do it while we're on the boat. It'll be relaxing."

Surprised, but delighted by Reny's change in manner, Piers relaxed. They'd spent the remainder of the evening laughing over old stories and past glories of their time at university.

The next morning, a strange flood of relief came over Piers as the reservation was completed. It progressed naturally to a feeling of excitement at seeing Helen. It would be a surprise for her, and he wanted to let Reny know they'd been successful at getting the reservations.

Heading downstairs to tell the lodge host they'd be checking out early, Piers stopped at Reny's bedroom door and knocked.

Redfern didn't answer, so Piers leaned inside hoping to find Reny and tell him they'd been successful in getting the reservations.

"Reny?" he called but receiving no response he hesitated.

A strong inclination to push the door further took over his natural English reserve. To his wonderment, he saw a suitcase open on the bed with an evening dress spilling out. He remembered Coraliss Redfern wearing it the last night they'd been together at Healy.

The sound of a shower running in the bathroom to his left caught his attention. Had Coraliss returned? How odd? Reny's story about his wife going to D.C. was still fresh in his mind.

Backing out of the room, Piers pulled the door shut. Continuing downstairs, his earlier enthusiasm for going to the hotel barge turned into a nagging feeling of unease.

If Coraliss Redfern was back, she would enjoy the trip up The Caledonian, he told himself, but if she *wasn't* back...

Why did that come to mind? He quickly tried to squelch his uncertainty. His brain offered some potential answers. If Coraliss is not here, then she probably left one of her suitcases accidentally. Reny's carrying it until he can return it to her. The simple, obvious answer is usually the right one.

But the feeling of unease continued to bubble, pooling in his mind and broadening in its scope. He instinctively knew he'd made a mistake, a critical error in judgment, and he'd compounded it by taking it to Helen.

Chapter Twelve

Friday
Marsden-Lacey, Yorkshire

The last cart of newly cut hops sat near the barn's open door. Polly Johns inhaled deeply of their sweet summer aroma. Fruity, herbal, and even a dash of mint, the hops' fragrance filled the barnyard and reminded her of how lucky she was to do what she loved best—make beer.

"If I could bottle this smell, I would," she said, her eyes shut and head back like someone in olfactory heaven.

Her eyes snapped open, and she laughed out loud, making her naturally cheery expression even brighter.

"What a ninny! I *do* bottle it and I make lots of money from people drinking it."

"If you don't quit talking to yourself, I'll put you in a home."

Spinning around, Polly saw her only son, Johns, mischievously grinning at her. She walked over and hugged him.

"I'd like to see you try. How's my boy? Would you like some lunch?"

He shook his head and leaned on the back of a cart holding the hops.

"Mum, I'd like some advice. Do you need some help with these?" he thumbed over his shoulder at the hops.

"No, that's why I have Dale and Terry. You come inside with me and have lunch. We can talk."

Polly's house was the quintessential English farm home. Constructed of stone and brimming with character, its charms were many. Every room boasted original exposed beams, beautiful stone mullioned windows, and stone flagged floors running throughout the downstairs. Upstairs, oriental rugs covered the polished wooden floors and Tudor oak paneling gave the house a warm, cozy, and timeless feeling.

In her kitchen, a long harvest table busy with cookbooks, crockery, and papers, sat near a wide bay window overlooking a green valley with Marsden-Lacey and the River Calder tucked among its hills. As Johns walked in he saw Martha's cat, Gus, and her dog, Amos snoozing near the Aga in the same bed. Polly pointed to the table and said, "Have a seat."

Johns did as he was told, and Polly cut hefty slices from a loaf of Rye she'd cooked the day before.

"So, out with it," she said, her tone direct. "What's going on with Martha? She wouldn't say much when she dropped off her fur children, but I could see something was bothering her."

"How did you know my problem has anything to do with Martha?" he asked, looking like Watson to Polly's Sherlock. "I could be here to talk about...something else."

"Well, you don't ask for advice from me about your work. Your only other interests are fishing, darts, and Martha. Since I've never talked with you about fishing or darts, it's got to be Martha. What did *you* do?"

"Mum!" he exclaimed indignantly. "Why do you think it's something *I* did? It was her. She practically called me a weakling, but I showed her. I finally put Adam Buchanan in his place."

Polly shot a quick side-glance at her son and drew her mouth into a tight bow. She turned around holding the long, serrated bread knife pointing up at the ceiling like a goddess of justice. Studying her son, she wondered if his bruised ego was self-inflicted or otherwise.

"Lovely, I hope it was worth it," Polly said sounding terse. "What exactly did Martha say?"

He looked down at a cookbook and played with a corner of its binding.

"She said Adam told her he could kill people with his bare hands. Pompous blowhard!"

"And?" Polly coaxed, returning to the loaf of Rye and sawing it with vigor.

Her son wobbled his head slightly from side to side and shrugged, obviously not comfortable repeating last night's conversation to his mother.

"She was worried I would get hurt," he answered, "and wouldn't see me anymore if I confronted Buchanan."

"Is that all?" Polly asked.

He sat across from her, looking dumbfounded.

"Is that all, mum?" he responded. "She implied I was less of a man than that pile of horse manure."

Polly cocked her head to one side and studied her progeny for signs of intelligence. She knew he was a smart man, a man who solved crimes and administered an entire office of constables, but when dealing with women and affairs of the heart, he struggled.

"I smell manure all right, but it's yours. No, Merriam, that is *not* what Martha said to you. She told you in so many words your jealousy scared her. Scared! Do you hear the sentence clearly now? She used the wrong psychology on you, I'll give you that, but she was trying to keep you safe."

Polly went on making her son his sandwich and put it on a plate. Sitting down beside him, she said, "I love you, dear, but you don't listen well, especially when it comes to the way women express themselves. Martha used the ploy of not seeing you anymore because it is typically the only thing left to someone when they fear their loved one, especially a bull-headed, ego-stung male, is about to get into a fight."

Johns looked downcast. He didn't pick up the delicious sandwich waiting for him compliantly on the plate.

"I've been a horse's ass haven't I?" he said lifting his gaze to his mother's face.

"What did you do after she asked you not to confront this Buchanan person?" Polly asked, pursing her lips tightly.

"I went inside and," Johns said taking a breath and letting it out, "laid him out on the floor with one punch."

A compressed, thin-lip grin spread across his face. She recognized it as the one he so often had as a little boy, as a gawky teenager, and as a grown-up man whenever he was too proud of his actions to not let his genuine personality show through. She shook her head and reached over to scuff the top of his head, a mother's loving smile pulling at the corners of her mouth.

"Well, I can see you're proud of yourself, but I'm assuming you need to get back into Martha's good graces, so my advice is to apologize and promise to be less of a hothead and more like someone she can respect."

Polly stood up from her chair.

"Respect?" he snapped. "Why wouldn't she respect me?"

"Because you didn't trust her when she told you she didn't have any interest in the man, you acted like a man who didn't have any confidence in himself by trying to prove yourself with your fists, and you told her by storming into the pub that her fear was secondary to your ego."

Her son sat in his chair with his mouth ajar, looking at her like she'd lit her hair on fire. He didn't speak for a half minute, but when he did, it was with a softness and humbleness Polly knew was always at the core of his nature.

"Thanks, mum."

He stood up and came over, wrapping her in a tight hug.

"I love you," he said to the top of her head.

"I love you, too. Go find Martha and make it up to her. She's not the type to put up with silliness."

Letting her go, he grabbed the sandwich from the plate and started for the door.

"Oh, and two more things," Polly called after him. "When you find Martha, bring her chocolate. It's a sure-fire way of letting women know you're thinking of them, you want to make them happy, and you like them just as they are; skinny enough to eat chocolate."

"And the second thing?" Johns asked.

"Good luck at the dart tourney!"

Chapter Thirteen

Saturday
Banavie, Scotland

M artha had parked the Green Bean in a lot overlooking the canal. In the distance, she saw Neptune's Staircase, a set of eight lock gates used for raising and lowering vessels along the Caledonian canal system in Banavie.

Ben Nevis, the mountain with its head in the clouds as the ancient Gaelic people liked to call it, dominated the skyline. Scotland's highest peak was true to its name today, hiding behind a thin veil of white mist. Something about Scotland made the soul quicken with excitement for what lay ahead.

"Do you see The Caledonian Queen anywhere?" Helen asked.

"Hmmm," Martha said, studying the canal for signs of a huge hotel barge. "Nope, sure we're in the right place?"

They scanned the area for barges, possible docks, and any signs of the boarding area for The Caledonian Queen.

"Hey, look over there," Helen said pointing down the canal. "I see it coming."

It was a magnificent sight to behold. A huge Luxemotor Dutch barge, her hull painted a lovely, deep Midnight blue and her deck-house a crisp white, floated serenely into view. The Scottish flag flew midship from its star pole, announcing her proud heritage.

"I'm so excited to see the inside," Martha gushed. "I bet we sleep like babies for the next week. Aunt Tilda said their cruise last fall to the Bahamas was amazing. She slept better than she had in her entire life."

Helen made a sucking sound.

"What?" Martha snapped. "Why did you make that sound? You always make funny sounds when I discuss Tilda."

Helen shrugged noncommittally.

"Your Aunt Tilda was probably three sheets to the wind and would have slept 'like a baby' no matter where she was," Helen replied with a giggle.

"You know," Martha countered. "My Aunt Tilda was onboard for a poker tournament. She never drinks the hooch and plays. Actually, that's her motto; Never Drink The Hooch and Play."

Helen laughed out loud and turned to face a grinning Martha.

"And a dang good one it is, too."

Quiet again, the two friends watched the boat come to rest along the long concrete docking area in front of them.

"Why didn't Tilda come over for Kate's graduation?" Helen asked out of the blue.

Martha sighed.

"She and Harvey Burkus, her boyfriend, you know he turned seventy-five last June. Well, they had a slight run-in with Jackie Boy Divine. He's the one who makes those fabulous wigs for Tilda. The story goes that Jackie Boy made Aunt T. a knock-out red job with lots of curls and rhinestones woven into the strands. She sent me a picture. It was amazing. Tilda was to wear it in Vegas at the poker nationals."

"Would have made an excellent distraction stratagem aimed at her competitors," Helen added nodding.

"For sure! Well, Tilda paid in advance, but when she and

Harvey went to pick it up from Jackie Boy, he didn't want to let her have it. He said it was his greatest creation yet, and he wanted to keep it and wear it himself for the annual drag queen competition in Miami, Florida."

"Sounds like a perfectly natural outcome between wig divas," Helen agreed.

Martha nodded soberly.

"It happens more often than you know. Well, I guess Harvey and Jackie Boy got into a slap fest and Tilda had to break them up. The short side of the story is Tilda threw out her back wrangling Jackie Boy and her beau, Harvey. She had to cancel coming to England to let herself heal."

"It's got to be true," Helen mumbled. "You can't make that stuff up."

"Hey, they've docked," Martha pointed out. "Let's get our stuff. I call dibs on the bed next to the head — that's a toilet in boat talk."

Soon, the girls were meeting the captain, Emily Tangent, a beautiful, Nordic-like woman in her forties with piercing blue eyes and a gentle manner. As they were the first guests to arrive, the three women chatted about the upcoming cruise.

"We will leave the boat for one day to conduct some business we have further inland," Helen said.

"That's perfectly fine," Captain Tangent replied. "What area will you be traveling to?"

"A private home near Invergarry," Martha answered. "An art advisor, also one of your guests, asked Helen to give her opinion on two sixteenth-century manuscripts."

"This answers the mystery," Captain Tangent said. "I wondered who the three people were from R&M Holdings, LLC. The manifest sent to us by corporate did not give us your names but stated the three passengers were with an art advisory company. Who is the third person in your party?"

"Sasha Pelletier," Helen answered.

Emily Tangent's face went white. Martha saw her jaw momentarily drop as she gripped the edge of the railing. She quickly regained composure and breathed deeply.

"I'm so sorry," she said, her face once again stoic and controlled. "I may have a cold coming on. Please excuse me and make yourself comfortable in the saloon. My chef has prepared some wonderful appetizers and drinks."

With a faint nod, Emily Tangent disappeared to the stern of the boat with Martha and Helen watching her go. The two women turned to face the beautiful vista of mountains and loch, looking like the stiff, female figureheads attached to the prows of Spanish galleons.

"She looked like you slapped her when you said Sasha's name," Martha whispered.

"I know," Helen whispered back. "There's a story there. It should be an interesting dinner tonight."

"Oh my God!" Martha gasped, reaching over and squeezing Helen's wrist.

"What? What is it?" Helen asked, spinning around to look in the same direction as her friend.

"I'm gonna faint, Helen," Martha breathed. "It's Eddie Wild!"

Helen looked at the middle-aged man walking up the gang-plank. Her face a study in confusion.

"Who's Eddie Wild?"

Martha answered, her tone sounding more like a teenage girl's breathless adoration for a pop star.

"Helen, only the most wonderful rock n' roll front man and singer-songwriter of all time and he's coming on this boat!"

Chapter Fourteen

"We're supposed to be on our honeymoon," the young, long-legged blonde said to Helen. "Eddie had a concert in London and his publicist recommended this cruise, so here we are. It's a perfect quick break before he plays in Amsterdam next week. I'd love a warm beach, but Eddie's always wanted to see Culloden. We'll visit there when we reach Inverness. He's fascinated with military history." She shrugged and added, "Fun facts about rock stars."

Helen studied Eddie Wild's girlfriend as she lifted the glass of sherry to her lips. Bella was an extraordinary beauty yet down to Earth in her attitude. There was a soft hint of a Texas accent, and her eyes were cornflower blue.

She wore a simple dress, no tattoos, and long, luxuriant hair that flowed freely down her back. Bella was true to her name and she would have stood out in any room whether it was this one or if it was an amphitheater with twenty-thousand people crammed together. It wasn't any wonder she caught the eye of Eddie.

"Does he find situations like this uncomfortable?" Helen asked. She looked over at Martha, who was obviously in awe of Eddie as she stood talking with him. "I mean, it would be hard being a celebrity."

Bella twirled the end of a loose strand of blonde hair between two fingers.

"Eddie likes people. He's been out of things for about seven years working on this new album. He's the most easy-going person I've ever met, but when he's writing or producing, he's so focused."

She looked over at him, a tender smile brushing her lips. The rattle of the saloon's doorknob announced a fresh addition to their party. Everyone, because of the hotel barge's intimate atmosphere, turned to see who it was.

Sasha Pelletier emerged from the doorway looking a bit bedraggled from the heavy downpour unleashing itself on Banavie. The steward helped her with her coat and once free of it; she gave Helen and Martha a wave. Coming over to where they were, she smiled and offered her hand to Bella and Eddie.

"Hello, I'm Sasha Pelletier."

Introductions went around and the guests reassembled themselves in comfortable chairs. As they chatted, Helen noticed Captain Tangent steal into the room unnoticed by anyone. Her expression was a mask of professionalism as she scanned the guests. Helen wondered if Emily Tangent was trying to decide which of the younger women was Sasha Pelletier. It had to be impossible to discern from her place across the room. Soon, Emily strode toward them.

Helen made the introductions.

"Captain Tangent this is Sasha Pelletier, Bella, and Eddie Wild."

She watched with keen interest Emily Tangent's rigid composure thaw as her gaze fell on Sasha. Swallowing visibly, Emily held out her hand to the Wild's. When she turned to face Sasha, Helen instantly knew the truth.

"I am truly delighted to welcome all of you aboard my ship, The Caledonian Queen. I hope your trip is most enjoyable and if there is anything you need, please ask my steward, Mr. Carbone. He prefers you call him Matteo."

The company and the conversation were sparkling. With each

person bringing a unique and diverse background to the party, the guests barely noticed the time pass.

The soft sound of a gong silenced the pleasant chatter.

"Dinner will be served in one hour," Matteo announced.

The guests, in pairs or alone, filtered out of the saloon. It was time to dress.

Helen followed Martha down the corridor. She was dying to ask Martha, once they were alone if she had seen Emily Tangent's response to meeting Sasha. With the door shut, she turned around to see Martha already stretched across the bed with her arms flung out on either side like she was about to make a snow angel.

"Oh, Helen, I feel horrible! I'm a terrible, terrible woman!"

She sat straight up again, her expression one of misery, and slumped forward, cradling her face in her hands.

"What are you going on about?" Helen asked. "Did I miss something?"

Martha pulled her face free from her hands and mashed them together in a gesture of prayer. Smudged mascara around her eyes made her look like an unhappy raccoon.

"I couldn't help myself, Helen. I was like a woman possessed by some crazed she-demon. I was in there flirting...with a man married to a gorgeous woman half my age. I'm horrible, wretched and sick, depraved human being..."

Martha flopped backward again and finished with dramatic flair.

"I've got to leave the boat."

Helen put both hands on her hips. In her wildest dreams, she never expected to have to handle a middle-aged woman's wild crush response to a rock star.

"Oh, for goodness sake, Martha, straighten up. You're reliving some teenage obsession. Get a hold of yourself. There is something much more intriguing I want to tell you about. I noticed another unusual reaction by Emily Tangent when she met Sasha."

Martha roused herself. Pulling herself upright again, she

blinked, her eyes sad, but hopeful about this tidbit of interesting news.

"What did you see?"

Helen came over to the bed and sat down beside her rumpled friend.

"Do you remember the woman in Agatha Christie's novel, *The Mirror Crack'd from Side to Side*?"

"I kind of do. Which woman?"

"The one who sees her past right before her eyes and kills the person who gave her son measles?"

"Oh great! I remember. Are you thinking she's a nut job who'd going to go around killing people?"

Helen rolled her eyes heavenward for help.

"No!" she snapped, shooting an irritated look at Martha. "You missed the point. I think..."

The idea seemed ridiculous, but how else to explain her feeling?

"I think," Helen mused out loud, "as crazy as it sounds, Sasha Pelletier is Emily Tangent's child."

Chapter Fifteen

The drive to Banavie from the hunting lodge would take a matter of four hours, but for Piers, it was feeling like ten. His decision to take Reny was eating at him, and the foul weather and curvy roads heightened his uncertainty.

Along the way, they'd completely abandoned the conversation about Piers coming on as an investor. Reny kept his topics to favorite soccer teams, his renovation work on the seventy-foot catamaran he kept in Monte Carlo, and what candidate he'd be backing in the next presidential election in the United States.

His two newest interests were collecting rare medieval manuscripts, and he talked about Helen's project near Invergarry, but Piers gently shifted the conversation away from the topic back to Reny's plans for sailing around the world.

The nuances of his pleasant chatter, if critically and logically inspected by someone, would have declared Reny Redfern to be an exceptional man among men, but Piers couldn't help feeling an uneasy, skin-crawling sensation at the nearness of him. He wished he'd never mentioned Helen's trip up the Caledonian.

Piers couldn't back out now. He'd already committed to going to the boat. Besides, he couldn't imagine spending another day alone with the man. Too many unanswered questions played at the corners of Piers' mind. Mainly, where was Reny's wife?

The suitcase with women's clothing Piers had seen laying on the bed in the hotel was not part of Reny's luggage when he brought his luggage down from his room this morning. He said nothing about forgetting a case, so what did he do with it?

During the drive, Piers' mind needled the mystery, unconsciously making his foot press harder on the gas pedal. As for Reny, he appeared the picture of relaxed, if not excited boyish enthusiasm for their trip.

Finally pulling into Banavie, they found the canal and The Caledonian Queen floating serenely along her mooring.

Rain pelted the Mercedes as Piers parked the car in the lot across from the boat. The two men quickly jumped out and grabbed luggage from the trunk. With a sprint to the gangplank, they soon found themselves in the warm, dry saloon of the hotel barge.

The steward poured two glasses of Scotch for them and they settled in wingbacks near the fire. Eager to see Helen, Piers hoped to have the drink and excuse himself, but as they talked, sipping the Scotch, a tall, slim, and athletic-looking woman in her late forties wearing a captain's uniform came noiselessly through the side door opposite of Piers. Reny, with his back to her entrance, was oblivious to her arrival.

Seeing the new guests, she smiled and came up behind where Reny sat. Piers stood and Reny followed suit. As the latter turned around, Piers watched the woman's congenial smile stall, blur, and twist into a grimace, finally melting entirely from her face.

"Nooo..."

The word blew from her mouth like a curse, and she stepped backward. It was as if she'd seen a vampire rise from a dark corner of her life.

"Why are you here? You're not welcome. You must leave."

Piers saw the woman's expression flit frantically from shock to fear to defiance. Reny, in complete contrast, was taking her surprising reaction with ease.

"Emily," he said, "*you* are the captain of this vessel?"

She only continued to look at him like he was a manifestation of an unholy thing. In a crisp tone, she demanded, "You must leave my boat at once."

Turning to Piers, she said, "I apologize for my...my behavior, but I have the power to ask anyone to leave."

"Do all your ex-lovers receive this warm welcome, Emily?" Reny asked.

"Only you," she answered.

There was no doubt about the tension between the two people. Piers took the opportunity and offered to give them privacy.

"This is a personal matter between you both." He turned to Redfern. "If you are fine with me looking for Helen, I'll see you at dinner."

Reny shrugged and nodded, much to Piers' relief. Turning away, Piers headed down the hallway, leaving the two verbal combatants behind him.

As he passed through the doorway, he caught Emily Tangent's last remark. It caused him to falter, and a shiver trickled down his spine. His last thought before switching over to looking for Helen's name on the cabin doors was, 'Hell hath no fury like a woman scorned'.

Chapter Sixteen

"Her child?" Martha echoed Helen's last words. "Why in the world would you even think of that?"

Helen sat still.

"I'll tell you why. I called Sir Alec to learn more about Sasha. She'd mentioned Alec when we talked. I always do a check on people I'm working with before getting involved with them. Sir Alec spoke highly of Sasha and they were close while she attended Cambridge. He became a surrogate father of sorts. Her adopted parents were older and had moved or retired to France."

Helen was thoughtful for a moment.

"Surely you noticed earlier how much the two women looked alike."

Martha shrugged.

"Something was distracting me."

"Um-hum," Helen acknowledged. "Well, they look enormously alike, and from Emily Tangent's behavior, she knows who Sasha is, too."

"Well, I hope they have a nice reunion," Martha said feeling irritable. "I need a shower and at least two hours to prepare myself mentally for dinner."

She rose, but Helen put a firm hand on her shoulder, pushing her back down.

"You're grumpy. What's the matter?"

"I'm tired. I'm too old to be giddy for long."

They both looked at each other and burst out in a short, good comrade laugh.

"That's for sure," Helen agreed.

"What the heck was I doing in there? I saw this idol of mine stroll on to the boat and I became a twenty-year-old groupie. I'm so embarrassed and yet I can't get the thought out of my mind. The man is sitting less than ten feet from this room. I've got to get this under control."

"It took you off-guard," Helen replied. "If Cary Grant had come on board, I would have made a total idiot of myself."

"Would you?" Martha asked, looking askance at Helen. "Well, yeah, I guess most people would. Merriam has thrown me for a loop with the way he's been acting over that puffed-up Adam Buchanan. I don't like someone putting fences around me. When I saw Eddie Wild, he reminded me of my youth, reminded me of that feeling of freedom, plus he's so gorgeous."

Martha gave one of the bed pillows a good punch.

"Don't beat yourself up too much, Martha. Eddie's probably used to it. Go out there tonight and be polite and be yourself. As for the situation with Merriam, you need to do some soul searching. It'll be fine. You'll see."

Martha sighed and smiled.

"Thanks, Helen. You have such a way of making things seem ordinary and simple."

Martha gave her friend a wrap-around shoulder hug saying, "And anytime you need someone to pull you up by your bootstraps, I'm your girl. Tonight, we'll have a good long talk, drink hot chocolate, and..."

A knock on the door rang out. Getting up, Helen opened the door to reveal a smiling Piers.

"Surprise!" he exclaimed, throwing his arms open.

Helen jumped into his embrace, and he lifted her off the ground, bringing her into the cabin.

"What are you doing here?" she asked after kissing him. "You're supposed to be with Reny."

He put her down and shrugged.

"I missed you too much."

Martha, sitting on the bed, watched his face.

"Come clean, Cousins. There's no doubt you missed her, but you look like a man who's seen some trouble. I can always tell. It's in the eyes."

Helen dropped on the bed beside Martha, a look of worry on her face.

"Is something wrong, honey?" she asked. "Martha's always right about her impressions, so tell me."

"Honestly," he said, "I've got the strangest feeling from Reny. If I told you, you'd probably think I was off my nutter."

"Not us," Martha stated, her tone matter of fact. "No stone throwers here, Piers."

He shook his head as if he wasn't sure where to begin. Taking a seat in a chair against the wall opposite them, he began.

"Coraliss Redfern's suitcase was in Reny's room yesterday, but she supposedly left for Washington D.C. a few days ago. He didn't bring the case with him from the lodge and when we arrived at the boat, the captain asked Reny to leave. Come to find out, he's an old lover and from the way she responded upon seeing him, you'd think he was the devil incarnate."

Helen and Martha sat nodding at him in silent unison.

"Weird, huh?" Piers asked and raised his eyebrows.

"It's been a heck of a day for Emily Tangent," Helen murmured.

"Yeah, a creepy ex-lover shows up *and* a long, lost child, all in one day," Martha mumbled as an addendum.

Piers' eyes widened at her statement. It brought back what he'd heard the captain say as he'd left the saloon earlier that afternoon.

"Maybe, that's why she said what she did."

"What?" the two women asked together, leaning forward, their eyes twinkling with curiosity.

"She told him, 'You've taken too much away from me, Reny. I'll see you burn in Hell.'"

Chapter Seventeen

S aturday Evening

BLACK TIE-WEARING MEN AND FORMAL GOWN-WEARING LADIES
were busying themselves at the multiple plates of hors d'oeuvres
when Helen, Martha, and Piers came into the saloon. Immediately
separating from them, Martha went to talk with Matteo.

Helen studied the room. The two newlyweds, Eddie and Bella,
were cozy on a settee next to the fireplace, their heads together in
intimate conversation. Sasha was talking with a new guest, a man,
near the bar. It occurred to Helen Sasha looked unsure about
something, but the sound of Bella's sudden, tinkling laughter
made her shift her attention back to the opposite side of the
room.

Matteo, the steward, came over offering bubbly champagne in
long-stemmed crystal glasses to her and Piers. Taking one, Helen
pointed Sasha out. The young woman excused herself from the
newcomer and walked over to them.

"Good evening."

"Good evening, Sasha," Helen replied. "This is my husband, Piers."

Sasha offered her hand and a kind smile to Piers.

"It's lovely to meet you. I'm delighted to be working with your wife and her colleague on this project."

"It's a pleasure to meet you, Ms. Pelletier."

"I didn't realize you were coming on the cruise. We will meet Mr. McMurray tomorrow. Would you like to tag along? If you've never been, the drive through the mountains is almost a spiritual journey."

Piers shook his head.

"No thank you. I plan to visit the Dalwhinnie Distillery with the group tomorrow."

Soon the three removed themselves to the sitting area to discuss the two Holinshed volumes. The newcomer, a Mr. Edwin Montfort, joined them. Helen noted his New Orleans accent, wondering if it was still his home.

He was asking Helen and Sasha about other ancient manuscripts they'd dealt with when Reny came over.

"Only last week," Sasha told them, "I enjoyed the privilege of negotiating the sell of a medieval Book of Hours."

As the young woman talked, Helen glanced up to see Reny's gaze boring down on Sasha. In his eyes, she read suspicion.

"What is your business in this project with Helen, Ms. Pelletier?" he asked, jumping into the conversation. "Are you working for a client?"

"I'm with Levine Art Advisors in London and I'm not at liberty to discuss the identity of our clients but I can say I've worked with them for about six months. It's been a mutually beneficial relationship."

Watching Reny's face, it occurred to Helen how wolf-like it was. He'd homed in on Sasha as if she was a rabbit, practically licked his chops. Angular, focused with teeth so white, Reny Redfern's face wasn't without a rugged beauty, but still, Helen thought, it wasn't one she wanted near her own.

"I'd love to come along with you to see the volumes," he said as if it was all arranged.

Sasha never flinched. Inviting Piers was one thing, but it was obvious Reny's interests were more mercenary. Protecting her client's interest was a priority. Inwardly, Helen was proud to see how Sasha maneuvered through the tricky situation.

"As delightful as it would be to share the volumes with others, at the moment I'm under agency with my client. Naturally, if they pass on these two works, I'd be happy to show them to you."

Not detoured, Reny asked.

"How did the volumes turn up? What's the back story? Will they be going to auction?"

Anyone within the group of five would have been hard-pressed to not feel a sting of awkwardness at Reny's overt and ill-timed pressure tactics. Helen watched as Martha wetted her lips, taking a tiny drink of her champagne. She knew that look in her friend's eyes. Sasha's backup was about to arrive.

"So, Mr. Redfern, Piers tells us Coraliss is in Washington D.C. It's a pity your wife wasn't able to join us. Does she have family there?"

Reny swung his attention from Sasha to Martha. He laughed, his cool, grey eyes flickering for a moment with annoyance. For a fraction of a second, his gaze rested on Martha's face. Helen noted the muscle at his temple quiver.

"Her father is Senator Anderson," he said more to the group than to Martha. "Coraliss practically grew up in Washington. I'm Swedish by birth, but as her husband, I've enjoyed living in the States for the last three years. I have offices in a few other countries, but my favorite is in New York."

Martha pushed on.

"I was reading something about Senator Anderson. Doesn't he sit on an important congressional committee?"

A steely glint shot through the grey eyes. A yellow flag of caution went up. It may not be prudent to know too much about

Reny Redfern's business or personal life. A true distaste for the man solidified in Helen's mind.

"My father-in-law serves on many important boards. I see little of the man. He travels a good deal."

"That's it!" Martha exclaimed. "He's on an aviation committee dealing with federal security and safety. Must come in handy."

Martha never flinched. Her smile was all kindness and curiosity, but she kept her gaze flat and firmly focused on Reny. Again, the same muscle in his jaw quivered.

"Yes, Mrs. Littleword, it is always an agreeable thing to have a senator in the family."

Matteo announced dinner, releasing the group from the tense circle of conversational chess. Name cards directed the seating arrangement. The guests found their seats. As the waiters placed the meal before them, people naturally talked among themselves, enjoying the food, the wine, and the company.

Captain Tangent was at the head talking with Piers. Across from Helen, Sasha talked with Bella about Los Angeles. Martha looked utterly delighted for she was beside Eddie discussing his second album from the 1980s. It occurred to Helen that was the reason for Martha's beeline toward Matteo earlier. She smiled inwardly.

Edwin Montfort sat on Helen's right side and they chatted for some time about New Orleans, beignets, the antique shops along Royal Street in the French Quarter, and the ancient Seven Sisters Oak in Mandeville. Helen was happy to hear the beautiful ancient tree was still healthy, and well-tended.

"I spent two years in New Orleans," Helen explained to Edwin. "My first job out of college was working for a book dealer in Royal Street. Do you still live in Louisiana?" she asked.

"Yes, and since my retirement, I've dedicated my free time to working with ecological teams trying to clean up areas impacted by petroleum spills. That's why I'm on my may to northern Scotland. I have a charity, R&M Holdings, which supports environmental issues. Years ago, a terrible accident occurred, practically wiping out the sea bird population and affecting the seal habitat one of the isles in the Shetlands. There is a group working to encourage rehabilitation of the area and I'm going there to spend two weeks."

"Admirable work, Mr. Montfort. How did the spill happen?"

The man sighed heavily as he cut the potatoes on his plate.

"I'm not an admirable person and it's not a pleasant story, Mrs. Cousins. I worked for a navigational software company in New Orleans for oil tankers. The tanker that went aground in The Shetlands was a ship we provided software for and I was the development engineer responsible for its malfunction. It was a default in the navigational system, and though I'd asked for more time to work out the kinks, there was pressure from the top to keep our bottom line profitable. Corporate greed at its worst."

Helen's curiosity revealed itself with her question.

"Do you know who was behind the pressure to use the software?"

Mr. Montfort nodded, not taking his gaze from his plate.

"Oh yes, I know," he said, glancing down briefly at the end of the table.

"Ten men died when the tanker ran aground, killing over two thousand birds, hundreds of seals and their pups, thousands of fish and even porpoises. The man and his minions responsible are despicable people, but what can anyone do? They're wealthy with lots of lawyers. Their argument would be they made their shareholder's bottom lines profitable. That's business, as they say."

He shrugged and finished putting butter on a roll.

"I'm sorry, Mr. Montfort, so many people and animals suffered at the hands of a few individuals' bank accounts," Helen said, feeling a loss of her appetite for the salmon laying on her plate.

"I, too, Mrs. Cousins," he said, his words like a muffled oath.

For an instant, he glanced down the table, adding, "Some people get away with murder and no *one*, no *legal system* ever holds them accountable."

Chapter Eighteen

"I'll bunk with Sasha," Martha said. "She has another bed."

She was trying to pack up her stuff and move out of the cabin so Piers and Helen could have a romantic evening alone.

With her hands full of clothes, Martha was kneeling on the floor trying to compress all her things back into her suitcase.

"I can't believe I managed to shove it all in here the first time."

"Why did you bring so much?" Piers asked.

She gave Piers a dry look, but a feeling of compassion stole over her. The two of them, Helen and Piers, were guilt-ridden enough she'd given up her bed so they could be together.

"You know I love you...both. I hope you have a cuddly evening together tucked into your bed drinking the champagne I stole from the bar and the bag of chips I snuck from the kitchen which by the way I stuffed in the closet in case Matteo comes in to tidy the room before bedtime."

"Is there anything not nailed down out there," Piers teased, thumbing in the saloon's direction, "you might have left behind?"

"Hey, Proper British Boy," Martha slung back while fighting a pair of black espadrilles into her case. "I'm not the one who's kicked a poor woman from her bed. Besides, you know you wanted that champagne but were too starched and tight-laced to get it for yourself. So, I cared enough to pinch you a bottle. Now, you can get Helen tipsy and have your way with her."

She gave Piers a finishing wink.

"Good Lord, Martha," Piers said laughing, "how can I make it up to you, imposing on your girls' week?"

Martha sat back on her heels and put her hands up in a gesture of defeat. Somehow what she packed had multiplied, and all the coaxing, prodding, or mashing wasn't working. From her place on the floor, she looked up at a bemused Piers.

"I'll think of something, Cousins. You can bet on it."

Helen sat unceremoniously on the bed. She was daintily filing her nails, her Mona Lisa smile revealing her pleasure at watching Martha and Piers fuss lovingly at each other.

"Anyway, it's probably best I'm in Sasha's room. That weird, psycho friend of yours, Piers, will probably try to harass the poor kid again. You might practice more discretion in who you run with. Where *do* you find your friends?"

"Hmmm," he mused, "lime kilns, kitchen freezers, utility closets, hospital toilets, gypsy boats, and..."

"Hush!" Martha said with a laugh. "Helen and I had no control over those situations. I'm talking about the lunatic you met in prep school and nurtured a relationship with over the years who is obviously a sociopath."

Piers leaned back on his pillow and put one hand behind his head. Taking the other hand, he laid it on Helen's back and gazed up at the ceiling. Martha continued.

"Helen and I are normal people, Piers, who've experienced unusual circumstances. Reny Redfern, so you may see the difference, is an *abnormal* person who gives people the creeps."

"I have to agree," Piers replied. "I didn't spend much time with him in school, but later he made a name for himself in the finance community. When he contacted me a few months ago about his plans to build better software for the aeronautic industry, it surprised me."

"I wouldn't trust him any further than I could throw him," Martha said standing up and wrapping her unwieldy suitcase in a bear hug. "He makes my skin crawl."

"Do you have everything?" Helen asked.

Piers stood up and attempted to help Martha and her feral suitcase through the door.

"If I don't, I'll get it tomorrow. Good night!"

As she made her way blindly through the cabin door, a thought occurred to her. Doing an about-face, Martha pushed back through, handing the suitcase to Piers.

"I remembered something," she said.

Muffled by the layers of clothing and nightgowns, Piers' voiced asked, "What did you remember?"

"What I read about Redfern's senator father-in-law."

Piers threw the crazy suitcase down on the bed, causing Helen to bounce from its sheer weight and prodigiousness.

"What did you read?" Piers asked.

"Senator Anderson is pushing the aviation industry to upgrade all of its new planes with state-of-the-art navigational software. Sounds like he's in cahoots with his son-in-law."

Piers, his expression was grim, sat down on the bed.

"If that's the case, I don't want any part of it," Piers said. "It'll blow up in our face at some point and cost us more in litigation fees than it's worth."

Helen was quiet. Martha noticed how contemplative her friend appeared as if she was putting an invisible mental puzzle together.

"What are you thinking?" she asked.

Looking up with an expression like she'd returned from a dream, Helen said, "I was wondering about something Edwin Montfort said at dinner tonight. He was a navigational systems engineer for a company in New Orleans. The story he told is uncomfortably familiar to your situation, Piers."

"How so?" Martha asked.

"A person with financial connections coerced his company into utilizing incompletely tested navigational software. It resulted in a horrific shipwreck, deaths of animals, men, and Montfort's company went bankrupt. Funny, but he kept looking down at the end of the dinner table as he told me the story. Now I remember who was sitting there."

She stopped. All three people stared at each other.

In unison, they said, "Reny Redfern!"

Chapter Nineteen

Martha dragged her case down the hallway and found Sasha's cabin door. Knocking softly, she waited. No one came. Once more, but still no answer. Taking the doorknob, she turned it and leaned on the door. It opened easily, soundlessly, revealing no one inside.

"Odd," she murmured, putting her suitcase at the foot of the bed.

It took some time to hang-up and put away her things. When she finished, she put on her nighttime attire and washed her face. The door opened and Sasha came into the room looking pale with eyes red from crying. Heading for her bed, she sat down and wiped her face with a tissue.

"Honey," Martha said, going over to her. "What is wrong?"

Sasha burst into tears.

"He's unbelievable!" she wailed and buried her face in her hands.

Martha, a veteran mother of a daughter, knew well how to handle most situations involving tears. She sat down beside Sasha and gently laid her hand on her forearm. The only thing she could think was perhaps Sasha had broken up with a boyfriend.

"Can I do anything to help?"

After some snuffling, eye dabbing, and allowing Martha to help her into her bed, Sasha became more subdued. She'd just accepted the hot cup of chamomile tea Martha made her when a soft knock caused both women to turn and look at the door.

Going over, Martha opened it, revealing Emily Tangent, her long blonde hair normally wound into a pretty chignon falling loosely about her head. Not looking at all like a boat's captain, Emily was wearing the oddest assortment of clothes and on her feet were tennis shoes.

"Why are you here?" she asked Martha, her words rushed.

Martha wasn't sure how to answer.

"Well, I didn't have a place tonight so…"

Emily Tangent brushed past her, obviously uninterested in Martha's answer to her question. She went straight to Sasha's bedside and knelt.

"Sasha, please forgive me. I've regretted every day of my life since they took you away."

Not sure of what to do and feeling every inch an awkward third-wheel, Martha moved toward the door to leave.

"Wait!" Sasha rang out. "Please, Mrs. Littleword, please say nothing to Mrs. Cousins about this."

Martha turned around.

"I won't, Sasha, but is there anything I can do to help you both?"

Emily lifted herself from the floor.

"I should leave."

But as she turned away from the bedside, Sasha reached up and took hold of Emily's hand.

"Don't go," she said, her words barely audible. "It's such a shock. It's been so long and I…I…always thought you didn't want me."

Her voice broke down as she began to cry once again.

Emily knelt again and put Sasha's hand to her face.

"Not want, you? You'll never know how much I wanted you. I've known where you were and who your parents were from the day they took you away. I was only seventeen. Your father refused to marry me, so I couldn't keep you. I was a blight on his future resume, I guess."

Emily Tangent broke down crying, her head cradled in the hands of the daughter she'd lost so many years ago. Helen had been right, Martha thought to herself as she slipped out of the door to leave the two women alone.

Standing in the hallway, she looked first one way and then the other.

"Where do I go now?" she whispered to herself. "There's no room left in the inn."

Chapter Twenty

Feeling underdressed for hoofing about the fancy boat, Martha was about to knock on Helen and Piers' door when she saw the saloon light come on.

"Maybe Matteo's around and he'll have some idea what's available."

Peeking in through the door, she saw Matteo putting glasses away at the bar. Martha made a throat-clearing noise. The young steward looked up. She couldn't help seeing how his eyes sparkled with amusement.

"May I help you with anything, Mrs. Littleword?" he asked.

Martha gave up any hope of retaining her dignity, after all, she was wearing her favorite pink, fuzzy robe and Garfield slippers. The ensemble went with her like a security blanket. At the end of any day, no matter how exhausted, uncertain, or even lonely she might be, she wrapped herself in their soft comforting warmth.

"Matteo, I've been booted from two rooms tonight. Are there any left unoccupied?"

His mouth compressed into a hard line, and he shook his head.

"We're full, Mrs. Littleword. Mr. Redfern took our last room."

The steward, normally so pleasant, looked as if he'd smelled something rotten at mentioning Redfern's name. Martha couldn't help seeing his reaction.

"Has Reny Redfern been a horse's ass to you, too, Matteo? There doesn't seem to be a person on board he hasn't inflicted some hurt upon, except perhaps Eddie Wild and his wife, Bella."

Matteo shrugged and gave Martha a sour grin.

"I don't know about that."

His tone indicated even Eddie knew Reny's bite. Martha's curiosity ratcheted up a notch. In a lower voice and shifting her stance, she asked, "Oh, come on, not Eddie, too?"

Matteo furtively scanned the room.

"I don't think in a million years Bella ever expected Redfern to walk onto this boat, or she'd never have set foot in Scotland."

"Why?" Martha asked.

The young steward, with his handsome Italian features, shifted his gaze to the floor. He shook his head.

"I shouldn't say anything. It's not my place, but I will tell you Redfern is the reason Eddie Wild's old record company dumped him. It's taken him almost five years to get back on his feet."

"Poor Eddie," Martha gushed in a whisper. She was quiet for a second, thinking. "I'm glad his career is back on track and his life, too. He looks happy and Bella is a wonderful medicine for him."

She offered Matteo a kind smile, but he appeared more down-hearted than ever.

"What is it, Matteo? Do you have feelings for Bella?" she asked, her words gentle.

Again, the shrug, making it clear to Martha he was definitely in love with the beautiful Bella.

"I was. I mean, we were. It doesn't matter!"

His last words becoming more heated, he looked up into Martha's face.

"Bella brought Eddie back from the brink. When his record label dropped him, he got into drugs. Bella was out in Los Angeles studying to become a clothing designer. She and I met there. We fell in love, but money was tight, so she took a job cleaning houses.

That's how she met Eddie. He was in the worst part of his addiction. She became his nurse, the driving force behind his comeback. Something in her wouldn't give up on him. I lost her. I don't blame Eddie. I blame the greed that ruined him."

Matteo's eyes flashed with anger.

"How does Reny Redfern play into this?"

"At the time, Redfern's finance company owned the media company Eddie was signed to. They dropped him because his last two albums didn't go platinum or gold. There's an interview with Redfern saying the music industry is at its best when its working as a money machine, not as a charity for has-been artists."

"How dare he!" Martha exclaimed. "Eddie Wild wrote some of the greatest rock masterpieces of the eighties, nineties, and his last album was fantastic. A has-been my foot!"

"Bella's love for Eddie is unusual," Matteo said bitterly. "But as long as she's happy, I'm okay."

Martha studied the young steward.

"You never said why she came up here. Did she know you were working on this boat, Matteo?"

He kept his gaze focused on the ground, tapping one foot nervously as if thinking before he answered.

"Bella and I have stayed in touch and I left Los Angeles last year and found this job working for the cruise industry. You see, The Caledonian Queen is only one hotel barge or cruise boat among fifty working across Europe. We don't know who our guests will be until the day they arrive."

Martha didn't push it any further. It was obvious to any woman Bella sought out Matteo.

"I hope this works out for all three of you, Matteo," Martha said, "but I still need a place to sleep tonight. Any ideas?"

He gave her a weak grin.

"If you'll give me some time, I may have one of the crew's bunks. Would that work tonight until we can work something out tomorrow?"

A touch of disappointment at bunking in a crew cabin mixed

with relief at not having to sleep on the couch in the saloon and a growing sense of exhaustion encouraged Martha to nod yes.

"I'll take it. Give me five minutes to grab a bag."

Slipping back down the hall, she tapped at Sasha's door and peeked in. Emily was sitting beside Sasha on the bed. Martha's immediate impression was of a reunion. They both looked up at her.

"I'm so sorry to interrupt. If I might have a minute to grab a bag, Matteo is putting me in another room."

"Oh, Mrs. Littleword," the two women said together but stopped.

They shared a smile at their in-sync response, but Sasha pushed on.

"You don't have to leave. I'd like it if you stayed. I feel we owe you an explanation."

Martha shook her head, her smile tender.

"No, you don't. This must be a surprising and emotional time for you both. I kind of got the gist of the situation, and if it were me and my daughter, I'd want some space to work through it all."

Emily, holding her daughter's hand, her eyes red-rimmed from the tears she'd spent in the last hour, sniffled saying, "Thank you so much, Mrs. Littleword. You cannot know what an emotional rollercoaster this day has been."

"I can't imagine. I'm sorry for what you've both suffered. I'll grab my things."

"No," Sasha protested and stood up, coming over to Martha. "Please stay here tonight. My," she turned and looked over her shoulder at Emily, "mother needs her rest and so do we."

"Okay, thank you. Let me go tell Matteo I won't be needing that crew bunk."

Both Sasha and Emily laughed.

"Mufidy, my mechanic snores terribly! You would have been better off on the saloon's couch. Stay here with Sasha. Those men down in the crew quarters wouldn't get much sleep trying to be on their best behavior with a lady sleeping among them."

"I am relieved," Martha said, with an internal laugh at how Emily knew Mufidy snored. "I'll be right back."

As Martha went through the cabin door, Sasha returned to her mother's side on the bed and resumed their conversation. Out in the hallway, one of Martha's fluffy Garfield slippers snagged the trim at the base of the cabin door. Struggling to pull it free, she caught the tail end of Emily's last words to her daughter.

"Sasha, I'm sorry you told him who you are. Promise me you'll not do what he asked. Reny Redfern is a dangerous man."

Chapter Twenty-One

Sunday
Loch Oich, Scotland

T he morning was glorious. During the night, the storm moved off leaving crystal clear skies and sunshine so cheery, The Caledonian Queen's guests were in excellent spirits.

A true Scottish menu of eggs, black pudding, bacon, pork sausages, and smoked salmon was spread across the buffet table, but these were just the beginning. For vegetarians, there was cheese, porridge, soda bread, and fried potato cakes. Also, Highland honey and wonderful clotted cream graced the diner's tables for toppings on the hot blueberry and orange scones nestled in pretty baskets. Only a dieter would be miserable at such a delightful and enticing buffet.

The crowd was chatty with one another and ate heartily. With the sun shining in through the long row of windows looking onto the mountains, the day ahead appeared full of promise and adventure for all.

The boat was underway toward Kytra, so the captain was not in attendance, but at her helm. Sitting by Helen was Piers on one side and Sasha on her other. Martha hadn't appeared and under the circumstances, with the food being so delicious and plentiful, Helen wondered at her absence.

"Where's Martha?" she asked Sasha.

"When I came from my walk around the deck, she wasn't in the cabin. I'm sorry. I don't know."

Helen noted the tightness in Sasha's voice. Looking as if she'd slept little during the night Helen put it off to nerves over today's upcoming negotiations and inspection of the Holinshed.

Piers' cell phone buzzed, and he excused himself from the table. No sooner had Piers disappeared than Helen's buzzed. She looked down to see Martha's number coming across the screen. Her message app showed Martha had texted three times since sitting down to breakfast. Putting the phone below the table, she read:

"Redfern's dead in your cabin!"

"Get in here!"

And another:

"Helen, I'm texting Piers!"

A quick intake of air causing a piece of scone to stick in her throat sent Helen into a coughing fit. The cell phone slipped from her grasp and fell under the table. As she stuck her head under the table to retrieve it, the rest of the guests stopped eating.

"Are you okay?" Edwin Montfort asked, his tone concerned.

"Mrs. Cousins, are you choking?" Matteo asked, coming to the table.

"Helen?" Sasha said, holding up the tablecloth and trying to offer Helen a glass of water.

Finally, with the coughing subsided, Helen retrieved the phone and reappeared from under the table, her hair mussed and her face as white as the linen.

"I'm fine," she croaked. "If you'll excuse me for a moment. I'm going to my cabin, be right back."

With a cool attempt to recompose herself, Helen brushed down her clothing and ruffed-up hair back into place, offering everyone a weak smile. They, in turn, regarded her with expressions of concern. Standing up from the table, she tried to gracefully sail from the room as if she was a woman still in possession of some poise, dignity and didn't have a dead body in her cabin.

Down the hall, she saw Martha's head peep out from hers and Piers' cabin door.

"Get in here!" Martha hissed.

Helen picked up the speed. Once within reach of Martha's grasp, she was pulled inside the cabin. Sitting on the edge of the bed, his face white with shock was Piers. At his feet lay the body of Reny Redfern.

"What the..." Helen cried. "He wasn't there twenty minutes ago."

She looked back and forth between Blanched Piers and Wild Martha.

"Who put him in here?" she demanded.

"Well, it wasn't me," Martha hissed. With a furtive look at the closed cabin door, she whispered, "Someone, probably the person who killed him, stuffed him in here."

"No duh," Helen retorted. "He's in OUR cabin. They're trying to pin it on *us*."

"Us!" Piers cried, levitating into a standing position and facing Helen. "Why us?"

Helen stood rooted to her spot; her hands flung out in a gesture of flabbergasted alarm.

"Cause he's your *friend*? I don't know," she tried to rationalize.

"I don't kill my friends, Helen," Piers retorted, his voice rising with indignation and alarm. "And he's not my friend. I've been rethinking my relationship with him."

"Really?" Martha hissed. "What does that mean, anyway? He's dead on the floor with a bashed-in head. There is no," she put her hands up and doing air quotes said, "rethinking your relationship as an excuse for murder."

"Okay, okay, calm down," Helen said, her tone low, intense, and rushed. "Piers didn't kill anyone."

"Thanks for the vote of confidence," Piers quipped.

Helen looked down at Reny. His feet were in the closet. Turning to Martha, she asked, "Was he in the *closet*?"

Martha shrugged.

"Yep, I was looking for something and he fell out."

Shaking her head, she continued to look at Reny.

"How long has he been in there?"

A tingle of horror zinged up her spine.

"Oh, please tell me, he wasn't in there all night," she pleaded, looking back and forth between the other two.

"No, I'm pretty sure," Martha jumped in, "someone stuffed him in there this morning."

"What makes you think so?" Helen asked.

"Well," Martha said, "with the boat moving around, you would have surely heard him in there."

Helen noted Martha's behavior was odd, but considering it was Martha, she pushed it out of her mind and jumped toward the proper response of finding a dead man in your cabin.

"We've got to tell the captain. Once the proper authorities take the matter in hand, they'll see Piers is innocent."

"I AM INNOCENT!" Piers exclaimed.

Dumbfounded, Helen went over to Piers.

"Darling, *I* know you're innocent, but after last night…"

"They will think you killed him," Martha said, flatly finishing her sentence.

"Noooo," Helen said, drawing out her word and looking at Martha. "I meant to say…"

She laid her hand on Piers' shoulder.

"You were with me the entire time. I'm your alibi."

Piers gave Helen a grim look, and said, "Let's not jump to conclusions or assume we know how the police will deduce innocence or guilt. I am innocent, plus I know a brilliant solicitor. Let's tell the captain."

Helen patted his arm.

"Okay," Martha said, "but I need to say this before we do. Piers may have wanted Redfern out of his *hair*, but he wasn't the only one. This boat is chock full of people who would've loved to see Reny Redfern dead."

Chapter Twenty-Two

The pilothouse of The Caledonian Queen smelled of linseed oil, coffee, and peat moss. The latter was burning in the tiny stove to keep the room warm, giving off its sweet scent. With its wrap-around windows, the pilothouse had an excellent three-hundred-and-sixty-degree panoramic view of the majestic Highland's landscape. Scottish Pines pushed up away from the banks of Loch Oich and quaint crofts tucked back into the landscape. It was a vista Emily Tangent never tired of seeing.

The Queen was entering another stretch of the canal proper. In about fifteen minutes, they would leave Loch Oich behind and head for the locks at Kytra. While Emily held a cup of hot coffee with one hand, the other lay gently upon the captain's wheel. Like a woman in a dream, she made small, intuitive corrections, keeping the barge comfortably cruising between the two broad banks of the loch.

She was quiet, thinking over yesterday's revelations and reunion with her daughter. It had been both frightening and thrilling. Terrified by Reny's arrival, she had no choice but to talk with Sasha. It was a classic tale of being between a rock and a hard place.

She could see Reny recognized the resemblance between her

and Sasha the minute he laid eyes on their daughter. So naturally, he cornered Emily to see if his calculations were right. Yesterday's conversation between them still made her nauseous this morning.

"Looks like you," he said, watching her closely.

She willed her face to stay motionless, free of signs of fear. It's what you do when a predator is sniffing for your weakness.

"There are lots of twenty-something women with blonde hair in the world," she had replied.

"No," he said like a cobra weaving and leaning in close, "that's the baby *you* gave up. I think Ms. Pelletier could help me pick up a few manuscripts I've had my eye on. She and I would make a brilliant team, conquer the art world. My money and influence, her client list. I think it's time she meets her real father. What do you say? Is it family reunion time?"

His words sizzled with menace, diving into her chest like a knife and pinning her with fear.

"I'd rather die," she said.

He roared with laughter and his eyes sparkled with glee. She remembered how he always loved it when he smelled fear on others.

"I think you mean it."

"Why don't you crawl back to Hell, Reny? Someday they'll string you up for your crimes. God knows there must be a few thousand horrors you've committed against humanity."

A snort of smug indifference was his only response as he disappeared toward his cabin before dinner.

Their conversation forced a hard decision. She needed to tell Sasha the complete truth. It was the only way to protect her, so she did.

As a smile brushed across Emily's face at last night's memory of talking with Sasha, the sound of her watch alarm brought her back to the present. Checking the time, she mentally calculated their arrival at the Kytra locks. The van would be waiting to take the guests to the distillery. Emily prided herself on maintaining a tight schedule of events for her passengers.

"Four hours," she said out loud to no one.

Furtively, she looked over her shoulder, making sure no one heard her talking to herself.

"I've got to quit doing that."

She mentally chastised herself for repeating the behavior.

The pilothouse's door creaked on its hinges. Someone was coming.

"Emily!" her head mechanic's voice called. "I'm coming up, okay?"

"Sure! Come up Mufidy," she answered.

The minute she heard his footfall on the last step, she turned around and waited. He took her into his arms, kissing her so hard, she dropped the cup of coffee.

Pulling free, she laughed.

"Look what you made me...," she said but didn't have the chance to finish before he kissed her again.

Emily's entire body went weak in his arms. Last night, she asked Mufidy to come to her cabin after talking with Sasha. He never left. They'd been more than colleagues for some time, but once Redfern appeared, Emily was grateful for the sense of protection Mufidy promised.

"I'm so glad you're here," she whispered against his chest. "Having Reny onboard has been horrible."

"If he comes near you again, I'll toss him into the Loch."

Emily heard the strength and protectiveness in his voice, something she'd never known before, and it filled her with warm peace.

"I'm more afraid for Sasha," she said. "He's threatening to turn her into one of his pawns like he does everyone. He wants to corner the art market and force her to do his bidding. I might need you to toss him in the loch if he goes near her again."

His laugh bellowed up from his chest and out into the air, proving he held no fear of Reny Redfern. Holding on through the turbulence of his laughter, she smiled to herself. He said, "Forget him. He's not worth the seagull droppings littering those benches along the canal. Let's get married, lass. I'll keep you safe."

His words stunned her.

"Married?" she asked, pulling back from him. "Are you sure, Mufidy?"

"Woman! I want to be with you in the open. I want us to build a life together."

She couldn't take her gaze from his eyes. So blue and so full of fire. A shot of pure joy sang through her being.

"Okay!" she said, reaching up and hugging him even tighter around his neck. "Let's do it!"

Quickly she looked at the bow, or front of the boat, to be certain of the vessel's position in the water. Jumping up, she planted a jubilant kiss on her new fiancé mouth.

Releasing him, she said, "Let's talk later. I need to get this boat to Kytra."

"Good, I'm holding you to it, Captain. By the way, Matteo's lost his keys again. We'll be going through the locks soon, and I went to get the windlasses. One is missing. Might need to pick up a spare in Fort Augustus."

"Matteo has been such a mess this trip," she replied. "His head is in the clouds over Bella Wild, the American girl married to the rock star. He's misplaced the keys, but he'll find them like he always does."

"Okay, I better go," Mufidy said. "I'll be up to relieve you in about two hours."

She watched him go down the stairs, but the door didn't bang shut as normal. Turning to check the bow again, she heard someone coming up the short flight of stairs.

"Mufidy? Are you back?"

Martha Littleword appeared instead.

"Captain Tangent," Emily noted the distress in the woman's voice and the worry-filled expression. "We've found Reny Redfern dead from a head wound. You need to come at once."

"Dead?" she asked.

"Definitely."

Checking herself to not smile, Emily tried to think. The next appropriate question popped out to her relief.

"Where is the body?"

Mrs. Littleword responded, her tone nervous.

"My cabin."

Emily repeated, "Your room? The one you slept in last night?"

She watched the shift from worry to confusion on Littleword's face.

"No, not the one I slept in, but the one I should have slept in."

"The Cousins' cabin?"

"Yes, but they'd been in their room all night. I went this morning to get some of my things from the cabin and I found him."

"So, what are you saying, Mrs. Littleword? Someone killed him this morning?"

"Or late last night."

Emily tried not to show relief, but it slipped, and she knew from Mrs. Littleword's expression, she needed to cover her mistake.

"You must forgive me, last night was so exhausting. I'm not myself. We need to contact Fort Augusta's police constabulary. Give me some time and I'll be down."

"Okay, we'll wait for you in the saloon."

Listening for the click of the door to be certain the Littleword woman had gone, Emily took her cell phone out and called the constabulary at Fort Augustus. She gave the boat's location and described the situation onboard. The constable told her to pull over, tie off on the bank, and follow protocol for a death. He explained an inspector would be there soon.

Mufidy and Matteo helped to bring the boat to rest along the edge of the canal. The entire process took almost twenty minutes. Once she was certain the mooring was secure, she went down to the saloon.

When she entered, the guests were sitting in chairs and sofas drinking tea or coffee. As she crossed the room, every eye moved with her. Their seriousness only inspired a weird giddiness within her, but she attempted to say something reflecting her capacity as captain.

"I'm sorry for this unfortunate event."

The words sounded hollow with insincerity.

"I must see...the body. The police will be here soon. We are docked and Matteo positioned the gangway, so you'll be able to access the towpath. I'm afraid we won't be continuing to Kytra until the police have given us the all-clear."

Moving quickly away from their gaze, she headed down the hall. Once at the Cousins' cabin, she turned and walked in through the doorway. There, on the floor, was Reny.

Her hand flew to her mouth to cover the smile of joy. The munchkins must have felt the same way when the house landed on the Wicked Witch of the West. Their song ran through her head. Forgetting her earlier self-admonition against voicing her thoughts out loud, she slipped once again and repeated the Munchkin Mayor's words, adding her own twist.

"This is a day of independence, Reny," she whispered as she leaned down over his body, "for me and *my* descendants."

Someone from behind cleared their throat, freezing Emily to the spot where she knelt. A searing stab of self-reproach sliced through her brain at her unfortunate timing. Shutting her eyes, she willed the words to slip back down her throat.

With slow deliberation, Emily rose, trying to steal herself, her mind burning as it worked to summon an explanation of her comment to the guest behind her. But as she turned, and her eyes fell on who was standing in the doorway. Her heart jumped in her chest.

"A day of independence?" the woman said. "Interesting comment. Let me introduce myself. I'm DCI Verity Moore of the Fort Augustus Police."

Chapter Twenty-Three

Helen and Martha sat together on deck chairs, looking out into the Scottish wilderness and sipping tea. Between them on a wooden table was a plate of croissants, Brie cheese, four pieces of homemade shortbread, and two gorgeous chocolate and raspberry truffles made by a master chocolatier in Pitlochry who supplied the boat with desserts.

Martha had assembled the plate with great care, even though Helen wasn't in the mood for eating. This was their typical response to stress: one hungry, the other lacking all appetite.

"Do you think the reason you're so thin is that you're stressed out a lot?" Martha asked as she lovingly bit into her first truffle. "It's something I've wondered over the last few years about you, Helen."

Looking at Martha out of the corner of her eye, Helen returned her gaze to Ben Nevis in the far distance.

"You're *not* stressed by a murder in our room?"

"Well, technically it was *your* room."

Helen didn't dignify Martha's insinuation with declarations of her innocence. Instead, because she was feeling irritable and worried, she flicked the edge of Martha's goody plate with her finger and said, "Where did you lift all this?"

Martha stopped sucking on her truffle and shot Helen a sour look.

"You're being snippy."

"You're being insensitive."

After the terse exchange, they both sat in silence, but soon Helen reached over and picked up a croissant and nibbled on it. Pouring Helen another cup of tea, Martha topped it off with a dab of honey, knowing, like a hungry, listless hummingbird, her friend needed a shot of sugar.

"Better eat some cheese," Martha added, "protein will help you from getting even crabbier."

Turning toward Martha, Helen's lips compressed in thoughtful consideration of the slice of cheese being offered to her and took it.

"Okay, but I'm not crabby. Why did you say that about the room being mine? That's kinda selfish if you ask me."

Martha was slow to answer, but after selecting a shortbread cookie and chewing on it for a moment, she answered, "Because I'm being passive-aggressive."

"Why?"

"Because I'm a butt."

"Yes, I know you're a butt, but why did you say it?"

"You know why."

"I don't."

"You do."

They were silent again, both chewing.

"You're mad because Piers is here, and you got kicked out of the room."

"*And* because this was to be *our* fun week together, and he came along with his stupid psychopath friend that everyone hated and ruined it," Martha finished.

They were quiet for a second. Both chuckled, exchanging grins. Helen reached over and patted Martha's hand.

"I can't help that Piers showed up. I think he wanted to be rid of Reny."

Helen bit off a substantial piece of the croissant and chewed it.

Not answering immediately, Martha's hand hovered over the plate as she appeared to be deciding between another shortbread cookie or the last truffle. After prolonged deliberation, she selected the shortbread.

"Well, we are certainly rid of him now," she said before daintily chomping into the cookie.

"True."

"Who do you think did it?" Martha mumbled.

"Emily Tangent has waited all this time to be with her daughter, but she hated Reny, and she was afraid he'd manipulate Sasha to get what he wanted from her."

"And he would have done so if he'd lived," Martha agreed.

Helen watched Martha swivel around in her chair, probably checking to see if anyone was within earshot. She continued.

"But it could've been Matteo or even Eddie Wild."

"Why them?" Helen asked, her interest and mood brightening.

"Last night I got the entire story about why Eddie Wild's career went in the dumpster and how Matteo lost the love of his life because of it. But there's something else I've been wondering. Did either you or Piers get into the closet this morning?"

Helen, one side of her cheek full of croissant and resembling a chipmunk, shook her head no. With a hard swallow and a drink of tea, she said, "It was your closet, so we didn't need to get into it for anything."

"True," Martha said taking another bite of her shortbread cookie.

Helen put her head into her hands mumbling something about wishing she'd never come on this trip.

Martha looked over at her.

"It's had some dark points, true, but the foods been great."

Helen swung around on her with wide-eyed indignation.

"A man is dead in my cabin!"

"Okay, okay. Settle down. Perhaps whoever stuck Reny in your cabin didn't mean to kill him. Did you and Piers leave the room between late, late last night and early this morning?"

"Not late at night, but earlier we went for a stroll up on deck to see the mountains and the moon. We took the champagne you... borrowed and drank two glasses in this very spot. The entire thing took forty minutes."

"No, I don't think that works. Too early into the night to put him in your closet."

"Your closet," Helen interjected.

Lowering her eyes to resemble an annoyed cat, Martha responded, "Okay, MY closet, but technically he was in *your* cabin. Let's consider the other suspects. What about Montfort? He could be the killer. He was shooting daggers at Redfern during dinner and you said he mentioned something about people who never pay the price for their crimes."

"That's an excellent point. Edwin Montfort losing his business, going bankrupt and wanting justice, had some great reasons for wanting Reny dead. Go back and explain to me what you were talking about earlier, you know, the part about Matteo and Eddie."

Martha took a sip of her tea.

"Matteo and Bella were a couple until Eddie came into the picture. The weird part is Bella's role. Why is she here? If she and Eddie are celebrating their wedding, why pick the one place she knows her old lover is working?"

Helen took a sip of her tea and pulled the blanket tighter across her shoulders.

"We should ask her?"

"Oh sure," Martha answered. "Why don't we wander over to a rock star's wife and casually say, hey Bella, you still in love with Matteo? Besides, their love affair has nothing to do with this."

"It might," Helen returned.

"It doesn't," came a woman's voice from behind them.

Helen and Martha's heads and bodies spun around to see Bella Wild standing there.

"Um…" Martha stammered, "we… were, well after talking about Matteo…"

Her words trickled to an end, leaving both of the older women looking guilty and shamed-face at the younger.

Bella sighed and came around in front of them. She leaned against the wooden balustrade and looked into the wind. It caught her long hair, caressing it with invisible fingers. Helen remembered having hair like that twenty years ago. She smiled at the pleasures of youth, but immediately remembered its pitfalls, too.

"Bella, why did you and Eddie come here?" she asked, her words kind.

"Because I don't know if I love Matteo still. Eddie knows it. I needed to see Matteo before Eddie and I get married. You see, the honeymoon hasn't happened yet. I came here to see if what I remembered feeling for Matteo was still real."

Bella's eyes misted over.

"Have a seat, Bella," Martha said, pulling one between her and Helen. "Would you like some tea?"

"I would, thank you."

Once seated and sipping from their cups, all three women stared off into the landscape.

"Why are you marrying Eddie?" Helen asked.

"Because he needs me. I keep him solid. I love Eddie. You have to understand that, but not the same way I loved Matteo. If you breathe a word of this to the media, I'll see you sued for everything you own," Bella said, coming up from her teacup, her eyes flashing with sincerity.

Martha put one hand up in a stop gesture and with the other hand patted the girl on the knee.

"Hold your horses, Bella. No one here," she pointed back and forth between her and Helen, "would ever, EVER do anything to hurt you or Eddie. For one thing, Helen doesn't need money like those people who sell stories to the media. She's loaded."

"Oh, for God's sake, Martha! Bella will think we're insane, or at least you are."

"Me?" Martha cried, indignant. "I'm simply pointing out that people who run to the media with their sordid stories usually want either a minute of fame or need money. Fame, you detest and money, you don't need."

Helen nodded like one of those bobble head people and turned to look at Bella.

"Let's go back to the original question. Why are you here, Bella? Oh, and one more thing, did you know Reny Redfern?"

Bella took a sip of her tea.

"Yes," she said. "Can I have a piece of the shortbread?"

Martha smiled and handed her one while Helen grabbed another piece of cheese. After everyone was enjoying either a shortbread cookie or a piece of cheese, Bella began her story.

"Eddie and I were to marry after his concert in London this week. I backed out and to be honest, he was wonderful about it. We had a long talk, and I told him the truth. He offered to come with me to Scotland to make sure I would be okay. We're like best friends and I know Eddie's hurt, but he understands. The shock was seeing Reny Redfern walk onboard. I knew Eddie wanted to confront him, if not kill him. He was so angry."

"Shhhh!" Martha hissed, looking around. "Don't say that too loud, honey. The police are everywhere."

"Oops, sorry," Bella said, "but it took everything I had to stop Eddie. We agreed last night, I need some time to myself, so Eddie's leaving the boat today."

"Leaving?" Martha said, not attempting to hide her disappointment.

Bella laughed.

"You ARE a fan, aren't you?"

"Who's a fan?" a man's voice asked.

All three women, like surprised turtles on a log, jumped in their seats. Fortunately, no one took the plunge into the Caledonian. Instead, they turned around to see a handsome Eddie Wild smiling down at them.

Chapter Twenty-Four

❧

"They want you to come back to the saloon," Eddie said. "We've all given our statements. Bella is next, and they'll want yours, too."

Bella stood up, giving Helen and Martha a pleading look. Its meaning was clear; say nothing to Eddie. He didn't follow her, but walked over to the railing, watching her go.

Excusing herself, Helen shot Martha a second silent reminder to play it cool. Though she knew she should follow Helen, she didn't want to. Starstruck, Martha had a colossal desire to have the first, and probably last, one-on-one moment with her idol. Not knowing where to begin, she stacked the teacups onto the empty plate. It was a way to buy time until she knew what to say.

"Are you traveling for work?" he asked her out of the blue.

It was weird to think of herself being alone with someone she admired so much. The teacups rattled with her anxiousness. Looking up, she saw him attempt a grin, but she knew his heart wasn't in it.

In that instant, she could see he wasn't a rock 'n roll idol anymore, only a person going through a sad and uncertain time. Being there many times in her own life, Eddie's fame, for Martha, dissipated like a fog when hit by the sun. He was someone real, someone deserving of compassion and respect.

"Yes, my colleague, Helen Ryes-Cousins, and I are here to assess a manuscript for Sasha Pelletier. Helen is a specialist in rare books and I'm her office manager slash best friend."

He nodded like he heard her, but his eyes were hollow as if behind them the heart knew too much pain. Martha put the plate and cups back down on the table. Wanting to help but not sure how, she took a tentative step in his direction.

"So, you know, I'm pretty sure you can trust me if you need to bend someone's ear."

He turned around to face her.

"Pretty sure?" he asked, his eyebrows slightly elevated, but his eyes smiling. "Why only pretty sure?"

Martha took a deep breath and sighed.

"I have what they call 'foot-in-mouth-disease'. I don't mean to hurt people, but I say exactly what I'm thinking. Lately, I've been working at not jumping in with my opinion on a subject until I've worked through what the other person may need first."

Eddie's bemused expression hastened Martha's attempt to explain further.

"Okay, okay, that didn't sound quite right."

She held up her hand.

"Let me try it this way. I'm trying to be more empathetic. It's part of the anger management classes I had to take..."

A look of horror spread across her face as she realized, again, she'd been a victim of her foot-in-mouth disease. Sucking in air, she resembled a red-headed blowfish with pursed lips. Shaking her head, she thought the best thing to do was walk away.

"Hey wait!" Eddie called after her laughing. "Martha? I have that same problem...foot and mouth disease."

Coming to a halt, she willed herself to plaster a smile across her face and spin back around.

"I'm sorry, honestly. I wanted to help."

Eddie's eyes were bright with humor.

"You wanna know what I thought you meant about trusting you?" he asked.

Martha cocked her head to the side but thought it better to not speak this time. She shook her head quickly from side-to-side.

"Well, people are always telling me I *can* trust them. Ninety-eight percent of the time, it's a lie. So, when anyone starts the conversation with that statement, I'm already counting the minutes before they ask for something."

Martha's eyes widened, and her heart sunk. Inside, she *had* wanted something. She knew fame put a vast distance between the Eddie's of the world and the Martha's. The idea of friendship between them was a naive hope in her heart, and better put away.

"I'm sorry, Mr. Wild," she said. "If you'll excuse me, I probably need to go give my statement."

"What did *you* mean?" he asked, his face and words serious.

She stood there holding the rattling teacups, her mind bloated with emotions and thoughts. There was nothing left to do. Martha let the foot-in-mouth disease run free.

"I meant I wouldn't hurt you for the world. You're like a best friend even though we've never met. Your songs went straight into my heart. It was like you were there for me and understood. I'm amazed at your courage and humor. I'm one of those people who'd protect my friends with my life and even though I may say something stupid to make you mad or hurt, I'd only do it because I'm an idiot not because I ever wanted to see you in pain."

A powerful impulse to jump overboard took hold of her.

"I gotta go. Thank you for your music, Mr. Wild."

Reaching over, he laid his hand on Martha's.

"It's okay," he said. "I hear that a lot from my fans and it is the best part of what I do. Thank you, Martha."

He gave her one of those honest smiles, and in his eyes, she saw the pain and uncertainty of his life at the moment. Wishing to make it better, she said one last thing using the same tone she used when her daughter needed reassurance.

"It will be okay. Bella loves you and your friends will be there always."

He looked uncertain.

"I don't know if she does."

"She does. She wouldn't be here if she didn't. You'll see. It's going to all work out fine."

He blinked and his mouth turned up into a hesitant smile.

"You seem to know more than you're letting on, but I'm not above having faith. Some days it's all we have."

"That and our friends," Martha added. "You know what helps me when I'm feeling down and unsure about things?"

"What?"

"Well, I listen to your music or I talk with someone who usually gives me a pep-talk and a hug."

Eddie took a deep breath and let it out.

"I'm a bit short on both today."

Martha forgot about the fame, the crush, and the distance between people.

"Come here," she said.

He shot her another look of uncertainty.

"Come on, I promise not to bite."

He chuckled and walked over to her.

Because he was so much taller, Martha stepped up onto the wooden deck chair and held out her arms. Bashfully, he came close enough for her to wrap him in a warm hug. Holding him close for a few moments, she patted the top of his spiky head and said it again, "It'll be okay, Eddie. I promise. Go down there and work things out with your Bella."

She released him with an encouraging smile and a wave. Walking away, he turned around.

"Thank you, Martha, for the pep-talk AND the hug."

"Any time."

Watching him walk away, her heart full of the milk of human kindness, Martha beamed at the back of a retreating Eddie. When it hit her brain, it was like a wake-up slap across the face. Bella's words came back to her.

"It took everything she had to keep Eddie from killing Reny."

A sinking, sad sensation took hold of her.

Achieving the entrance, the rock icon turned around and offered Martha a smile and a thumb's up gesture which she returned, but half-heartedly as he descended the stairs and out of view.

"Crap," she muttered out loud and stomped her foot. "Eddie Wild, you better *not* be Redfern's killer. I couldn't take it."

She shook her head from side to side.

"I just couldn't take it."

Chapter Twenty-Five

"I can't talk any louder," Piers said, cupping his cell phone to shield his words from eavesdroppers. Huddled in the corner of an alcove at the entrance to the saloon, he'd called Johns to solicit his advice. The Caledonian Queen was in turmoil. They'd hit an iceberg with Reny's murder, but the situation had, if it was possible, taken an even greater turn for the worse.

"Would you come over to the boat and talk with the inspector? I'd call my solicitor, but I thought you might have a better understanding of police matters. We're in a real pinch."

Johns, on the other end of the call, wondered if murder and mayhem had attached themselves permanently to Martha and Helen the same way cat hair always clung to the seat of his pants no matter how careful he was when he sat down at his mom's house.

"Let me guess," he said to Piers. "They found either Helen or Martha's fingerprints on the murder weapon."

The lengthy pause on Piers' end told Johns he was dead on.

"Probably Martha's," Johns added, sounding glum.

"Well, actually it was Helen's," Piers replied. "The person who killed Reny must have reached for whatever was conveniently available."

"Which was what?"

Piers sighed and answered.

"Her travel steamer."

"Her travel steamer?" Johns mused out loud. "Not exactly premeditated murder. Who wanted Redfern dead?"

"That's the interesting part of the story. Almost everyone on this boat," Piers replied, his tone flat.

"Including you?"

Loud and clear, Piers' hesitation came through the phone line in the form of his silence. His answer, to Johns who'd spent a professional lifetime listening for guilt, rang true.

"I'll be honest, the last few days with Reny were sour ones. He was pushing for my involvement as an investor in his new venture. Something about it didn't feel right. Also, his wife never showed up for our hunting holiday. She'd supposedly gone to D.C. to see her father."

Piers stopped his enumerations of Reny's faults, pausing for a long moment. His voice was low when he spoke again.

"There's more to our situation than I'm comfortable talking about on the phone."

"I leave this competition," Johns said, "and I won't be able to show my face in Marsden-Lacey ever again. We are in the last round this afternoon for league champions in our division and Alistair has been talking smack with Roddy Linston. They've wagered a bottle of Glenfiddich 40-Year-Old Single Malt Scotch Whiskey on the outcome."

"That'll set him back at least four grand."

"Yeah, if I leave, Perigrine will kill us both."

"I understand," Piers said, sounding glum. "Any words of advice?"

"Do what the inspector asks. You're in expert hands. They won't cart Helen off to jail today. Anyone could have picked up the steamer and hit the man. The investigating team knows it, too. As for me, darts should be done by around five o'clock and I will drive over afterward the pictures are taken. I need to talk with Martha, anyway."

"Okay," Piers said. "I'll keep you updated."

A stinging thought arrested Johns' movement from tapping the red icon to end the phone call.

"Hey, Cousins! You still there?" he called.

Piers' voice replied, "Yes? Is there something else?"

Nodding vigorously even though there was no one there to see, Johns said, "Yeah, there is something else. It is Martha and Helen. Keep an eye on them."

There was a brief pause on Piers' end of the line.

"Well, I am...," he sounded uncertain of Johns' meaning. "Is there something else I should know?"

"Just what I said. It's Martha and Helen. Keep a tight line on them. If things get dicey and it looks like the police might take Helen into custody..."

"Into custody?" Piers parroted back, interrupting Johns.

"Yes, into custody," Johns repeated, his tone instructive. "Knowing those two, they're likely to do a runner and that could be a problem, Cousins, a really big problem."

Chapter Twenty-Six

"We need to get you out of here," Martha whispered into Helen's ear as they sat on a narrow public bench along the canal's towpath. "I heard one of the police constables say the murder weapon was yours."

The Caledonian Queen, tethered to massive metal cleats, rested quietly, indifferent to the hustle and bustle of the humans upon her deck. She was a crime scene with plenty of yellow tape to prove it.

Detective Chief Inspector Verity Moore gave the guests leave to stretch their legs until the forensic team was finished. Their trip up the Caledonian was over until all questioning was finished.

"We are *not* going on the run," Helen practically growled. "Of course, the murder weapon is mine. I brought it with me to steam my clothes, then I thought I'd kill someone with it. I'm innocent! If we run, then and only then will I look guilty."

"Ever been in a women's prison?" Martha asked, keeping her voice low.

"No, have *you?*" Helen replied with a regal emphasis on the word you.

"No, but when I was about sixteen, I worked in a pet food

factory with a woman who went to prison for training a chimpanzee to hold up a bank. Her name was Belinda Sue Ripley."

"Uh, huh, okay, I'll bite. How in the world did she get her hands on a chimpanzee?" Helen asked, though not sure she wanted the answer.

"Her daddy had one of those drive-thru wild safari businesses. Belinda Sue grew up taking care of the animals. She'd dress Chester, that was the chimpanzee's name, in this cute cowboy suit with a two-gun holster. He only had cap guns, but they looked real. Every Christmas Chester was in the parade dressed as Santa and riding his donkey, Dale, who had these horns made from felt with sleigh bells around his neck. Chester threw candy. It was always a hit with the crowd."

Helen sat still. She sighed. It was better to let Martha finish the story than to fight against the tide. With encouragement, she might finish quicker.

"So, why did Belinda Sue have Chester rob a bank?"

"The idea came to her one day when she and Chester went to fill the car with gas out on the interstate where it was always cheaper."

"And?"

"According to Belinda Sue, a creepy man came over to her car as she pumped gas. To get him to leave, she told him her chimp carried a gun. At first, the guy thought she was bluffing and leaned through the car window to grab her purse, a stupid move on his part. Chester pulled Belinda's real gun from under the front seat and pointed it right in the man's face. Belinda said he nearly soiled himself trying to scramble back out of the window. That's when she realized Chester's potential and planned the bank job."

Helen kept her gaze steady upon Ben Nevis.

"Did she give him a real gun to use?" she asked, her tone rife with incredulity.

"I asked that question, too," Martha answered nonplused by Helen's offended state. "She dressed him in his Santa suit and sent him in with a real gun, not loaded of course. Belinda wouldn't hurt a fly."

"I suppose someone in the bank got wind of the fact the chimp wasn't acting alone," Helen asked.

"Exactly. Belinda Sue served fifteen years as an accessory to a bank robbery. They put Chester in a zoo, poor fellow. When I worked with Belinda at the pet food factory, she would tell me stories about being on the inside. It was a tough place, Helen. You'd be better off making a run for it until they find the killer. You're not gonna last long in prison."

Sometimes it was weird how Martha's insights worked on Helen's imagination. A flicker of worry for what might befall her if she did end up in a holding cell took root in her mind.

"Surely, I could post bail or whatever the system is here in Scotland."

"Maybe," Martha mused, but not sounding confident. "What if they don't find the killer? They'd need to convict someone, don't they? They might enjoy pinning it on an uptight, well-dressed, rich woman. You could be on that reality show, *I Was Innocent: Twenty Years Later*."

The knot Helen had been living with inside her stomach tightened. She scanned the upper deck of The Caledonian Queen, noting the police officers and forensic personnel.

"I'll take my chances with a good solicitor. Piers is working on it," Helen said. "Besides, all you are doing is scaring me, so hush."

Martha was quiet for the time it took for the detective inspector to appear on deck, walk over to the balustrade, and dial her cell phone.

"Who do you suppose she's talking to?" she asked.

"It's probably her supervisor."

The inspector's words easily carried over to where the two friends sat. Helen was right the woman was talking with someone further up the police food chain.

"She had motive," they heard her say. "They may have been involved, there was a heated exchange, and one of the crew claims she'd threatened him. I think we have probable cause. I'd like to make an arrest."

"They don't think it's you," Martha whispered. "I bet she's talking about Emily Tangent."

Feeling a wave of sickness well up within her, Helen turned to Martha with a look of panic. Reaching for her friend's hand, she said, "Not Emily, Martha. It's got to be me. The inspector is talking about me."

Chapter Twenty-Seven

"Noooo," Martha countered. "It can't be you. You haven't gone near Reny except for meals."

Helen shook her head and gripped Martha's hand tighter.

"You don't know everything. Early last evening I had a frightening run-in with Reny," she said. "He must have known Piers went on deck to try for a better signal to call New York. You were in Sasha's room and I was in the shower. Reny came into the bathroom."

Helen put her face in her hands.

Martha was thunderstruck.

"That sicko! Helen, tell me he didn't try anything..."

Shaking her head back and forth, Helen quickly replied.

"No, but Martha, he said *nothing*. It was like something out of an Alfred Hitchcock film. The bathroom was filled with steam, and he just stood there. I thought at first it was Piers, but when he never spoke, I turned around and saw who it was. It scared me to death, and I yelled at him, telling him to get out."

"Did he?"

"Oh yes, but with no attempt to hurry. It was so, so frightening."

"Did you tell Piers?"

Martha watched Helen's profile and knew the answer without her response.

"I told him. He was so angry it took every argument I had to keep Piers from confronting Reny."

Trying to process this fresh revelation, Martha was silent for a moment. She didn't want to ask the obvious question, but she had to.

"Did Piers kill him?"

Helen turned her head quickly to face Martha, her expression a stone-cold steeliness.

"Of course not! Last night and this morning, he was with me the entire time. I was the one who went back to my room to grab my sweater before breakfast this morning. Piers was always ahead of me."

Martha swallowed hard. Like a person who was losing her voice, her next words crackled with fear.

"You've been a cool customer all morning, Helen, not mentioning any of this. Why do I get the feeling Reny came into your cabin again when you went back for the sweater?"

For a moment, Helen didn't speak. Martha saw her friend wrestling with what to say. When it came, her answer was barely audible.

"Yes, he did."

Like a diving bell, Martha's heart sunk.

"Helen, please tell me it wasn't you."

"Of course not. He wanted me to get him the manuscript we are examining at McMurray's today and offered me an insane amount of money to do so. I told him no and to get out. He turned and went to the door. I thought he left, so I turned to go into my bathroom when he came up behind me. He grabbed me around the waist, and I think because of what happened the night before, I lashed out with my hand. I told him to get out and that he wouldn't see a dime from Piers for his stupid company. The marks along his face, I did that, but I didn't grab the steamer. When I left, I passed Matteo in the hall. He must have heard what I said, but I swear Reny was fine."

Helen's voice crescendoed, but Martha stalled its rise by applying firm pressure to her arm.

"Lower your voice," she said. "They will find the DNA from his face wounds match yours."

"I know!" Helen cried, squeezing Martha's hand so tight it hurt. "I will go to jail for that evil, horrible man's murder and it wasn't me."

Turning to look Martha squarely in the eyes, she added, "If it has to be someone, I'd rather it be me than Piers. They'll be kinder to me, won't they? Surely everything you said about women's prison won't be as bad as it would be at a man's?"

"Did you tell the officer who took your statement about Reny coming into your room and you hitting him?"

Helen shook her head no.

"Something made me stop. I didn't want to put the noose around my neck or Piers'. This entire morning, I've been trying to figure out who was in the hall, who wasn't at breakfast, and measuring each person's motives against everyone else's."

Numbness slowed Martha's ability to think through all the scenarios logically. The distance from what she had believed ten minutes ago to what she knew now was nothing short of quantum in its scope. Helen, the most unlikely of all the people on board The Caledonian Queen to kill Reny Redfern, was the prime suspect.

It was as if someone had taken full advantage of the argument they'd overheard between Helen and Reny. They must have waited for Helen to leave, slipped inside, and killed him.

The worst part was Helen had multiple motives. Even though a solicitor could argue she acted out of anger or even self-protection, she committed a terrible infraction; she lied to the police. Martha's instinct was never wrong. Helen would go to jail, and it would be an open and shut case against her.

"I was right," she said low but firm.

"Right?"

"We definitely need to get you out of here."

Chapter Twenty-Eight

❧❀❧

"**B**ut I'm expected at twelve-thirty for my meeting outside Invergarry. We would happily take an officer along to guarantee our return."

With little success, Sasha was pleading for DCI Moore's approval. They would complete the meeting with Mr. McMurray, she argued, including Helen's time to assess the manuscript in less than a few hours.

"Unless you intend to make an arrest, we should be free to go about our business," Sasha said.

Moore's Cheshire cat smile gave nothing away. A woman of about fifty years, she'd spent the first half of her professional life within a man's world learning patience and fortitude, the second half she'd perfected being one step ahead of everyone else. Sasha Pelletier's bravado regarding her right to go about her business was little more than the buzzing of a midge fly in the inspector's ear, slightly irritating and with no actual threat.

"You will stay put until we finish the statements," she replied.

"Helen Cousins, Martha Littleword, and I finished an hour ago. Why should we need to wait?" Sasha pushed.

The rebuttal was pedantic in tone.

"Because, if someone tells us something, we find particularly intriguing, say, for example, about your movements, Miss Pelletier, we want the option to talk with you again today."

Moore watched the younger woman squirm. People's behavior fascinated her. A long time ago, she would have been more accommodating, even empathetic, but the first twelve hours after a murder was the most critical.

Gathering every detail of these people's lives, their interactions with one another, and their motivations were more important than handling their feelings with kid gloves.

"DS McBride will finish the last statement soon. I'll be able to tell you something after he's done," Moore said with disinterest.

With obvious frustration, the younger woman walked away, leaving Moore alone. Taking in her surroundings with a keen eye, she zeroed in on the two women sitting on the bench whispering to one another.

The dark-haired one was Helen Cousins, and the redhead was Martha Littleword. Colleagues and friends, their interests were intensely mutual. She watched their mannerisms. Upset, worried, and probably discussing something they hadn't revealed in one of their statements, Moore wished she read lips.

"Ma'am?" DS McBride's voice called from the saloon door's entry causing her to turn her attention away from the two women.

"Yes?"

"Will you please sit in on this last statement before it goes any further?"

This grabbed her attention completely.

"From that smile on your face, McBride, you must have a tidy piece of information."

The detective sergeant, new to his rank, smiled brilliantly.

"Kinda changes things, ma'am."

"I'll be right there."

Turning back around, Detective Chief Inspector Moore considered the two women furtively stealing glances back at her. Inwardly, she smiled. Helen Cousins was her number one choice for the murderer of Reny Redfern. Everything pointed at her.

She had motive, they'd found her prints on the murder weapon and no one else's, and the boat's steward overheard her threaten Redfern. Helen Cousins was facing a charge for assault or even murder.

Down the rabbit hole into the saloon where the statements were being taken, Moore saw McBride sitting across from the boat's head mechanic, Lewis Mufidy.

Taking a seat across from Mufidy, Chief Moore read the detective sergeant's notes. The room was quiet until she spoke.

"Mr. Mufidy, it says you've turned over a windlass for opening the canal locks. You found it on the deck at the stern of this boat near the galley. The windlass was caught in one of the water drains. What made you bring it to our attention?"

"It shouldn't have been there, and I'd gone to tell chef we wouldn't be needing dinner tonight since you'd moved the entire party to an inn. I've trained my eye to see anything out of place. It's what a good mechanic knows to do. The windlass was up against the gunwale as if someone had kicked it or thrown it in hopes of it sliding through the gunwales drainage hole which dumps overboard into the canal."

"You picked it up?" Moore asked with a hint of encouragement to prod him to tell more.

"No, that is I meant to pick it up, but when I bent over, I saw the hair and blood, so I went to find an officer."

Moore shook her head. This confused things terribly and slowed down her original intention for a finished case against Helen Cousins.

"How many windlasses does The Caledonian Queen have onboard?" she asked Mufidy.

"Five. The other four are accounted for in the place we keep them which is in a chest mounted to the boat's deck. It holds cleaning products, paint, flares, basic things needed on a boat."

"Who has access to the chest?"

"Only crew. It's kept locked at all times for safety. Crew members keep keys on their person at all times."

Moore sighed and stood up.

"Any of the crew report their keys missing?"

Mufidy looked down at his hands, drew air into his lungs and let it out. It was apparent he didn't want to name names. Shaking his head back and forth, he was quiet. When he spoke, it was with irritation.

"Redfern was a bad egg. He'd ruined lives. The world's a better place for him being gone."

Moore lowered the boom.

"Mr. Mufidy, we aren't here to decide the value of life with or without Reny Redfern in it. I need to find the person who killed him and turn that individual over to the procurator fiscal. What they do with the person is their business. Mine is to catch a killer, so I'll ask you again. Did any of the crew have their keys go missing in the last twenty-four hours?"

Lewis Mufidy swallowed, and with slow deliberation cleared his throat.

"Only one, the steward, Matteo."

Chapter Twenty-Nine

"Helen! Martha!" Sasha called. "We're cleared to go meet with Mr. McMurray!"

Turning around in tandem with Helen, Martha saw the pretty, young art advisor hurriedly coming up the towpath toward them.

"DCI Moore said as long as we check into The Highlander Hotel by tonight, we may go."

The two older women waited for the younger to arrive. With Sasha's face beaming with hope, a wisp of a memory caught at Martha's heart. Her daughter when she was a child, would run toward her the same way, her face bright with happiness. Youth's joie de vivre was a welcomed ray of sunshine along life's twists and turns.

Both Helen and Martha smiled in a tender, encouraging way as Sasha finally bridged the distance between them.

"I'm surprised we have the chief's okay to go," Helen said.

"They've found another murder weapon. It needs to go to a lab for analysis, so in the meantime, we can take care of your assessment," Sasha breathed more than said.

Helen and Martha shared a flash of unspoken understanding.

"Another murder weapon?" Martha asked.

"That's what Matteo told me. Someone took his staff keys and borrowed a windlass from the deck chest. Mufidy found it and it had bits of..."

Sasha's words dried up. It was as if the truth of her words only became real as she was uttering them. A look of fear and revulsion wiped the color from her face.

"It's horrible," she whispered.

The earlier energy evaporated from Sasha's countenance and she turned her gaze to the ground. With slumped shoulders, her whole being appeared to deflate. Finally, she looked back up at Helen and Martha, her expression full of anxiety.

"I need to go to this meeting. I need something normal. My work is the only thing that feels real, the only thing keeping me solid. I've made promises to my clients and my new boss. I can't afford another mess-up."

Neither Martha nor Helen said anything for a moment, but something about last night came back into Martha's mind.

"Sasha, did Reny mention anything to you about being your father last night? He showed a great deal of interest before dinner in the work you do. I got the feeling from Redfern he was a man who knew how to take advantage of his resources."

A paleness swept across Sasha's face. She looked down at the ground and the back up at them.

"Last night, my mother," she flashed a tentative smile, "Emily told me about him. I think he's possibly been a client of mine in the past. He might even be the reason I'm working at this new firm. You have no idea what my last twenty-four hours have been like."

Tears filled Sasha's eyes, and a trembling took hold of her. It was clear she was under great emotional distress. Helen crossed the distance. She wrapped the girl in her arms.

"It will be okay, Sasha," Helen soothed. "Do you know for sure it was Reny?"

The girl's head shook back and forth.

"No," she said.

When Sasha reemerged from Helen's hug, she wiped her face with a handkerchief offered by Martha. They guided her to a nearby bench.

Helen asked, "Tell us why you think he was a client of yours?"

"When I was still at Fordham's, the company before Levine's, my director, Louisa, came in one morning saying someone had requested me by name. She gave me the contact information of a personal assistant for a company in New York and told me to call. I did and I spoke with a woman named Alisha who told me a rare Swedish atlas by Cornelius Wytfliet was coming up for auction. Her boss wanted me to help with the purchase. The map would be for their company's private collection. She gave me details, I flew to New York and worked with a specialist to confirm the authenticity."

"Who was the expert you worked with in New York?" Helen asked.

"Henri Mercier. He's excellent."

"Yes, Henri is top-notch. What did he tell you?"

"He told me he wouldn't touch the atlas with a ten-foot pole."

"He thought it was probably hot?" Martha asked.

Sasha nodded.

"So, I called my director, Louisa, and told her my concern. I don't know what happened, but Louisa got very touchy with me and told me to go through with the purchase. She said nothing was in the art theft databases regarding the atlas."

"Did you?" Helen asked.

"No, and when I didn't, Louisa called me in New York saying the client was furious I'd cost them time and money. She flew to New York and handled the sale herself. Fordham's let me go and I paid for my flight home."

"What did the atlas go for?" Martha asked.

"Over four-hundred-thousand dollars. I called Henri after I got home to London and asked if he knew who purchased the atlas. He told me he didn't know. Auction houses are closed mouth about their buyer's identities, but Henri was told Louisa was with a young blonde woman with curls who won the atlas."

"Coraliss Redfern!" Helen exclaimed. "It has to be. That was Reny's area of expertise. He loved maps. She must have been buying it for him."

"I've never met her, so I don't know, but not three days later, I got a call from my current firm asking me to come for an interview. It confused me because I'd never even sent them a copy of my CV. They told me this R&M Holdings wanted me personally to handle their business. Until three days ago, I thought it was because of my integrity over the Wytfliet atlas, but as of last night, I know that was never the case."

"What do you mean?" Martha asked.

Sasha sighed and her shoulders drooped once more.

"Before Emily and I talked, I went to see...my father."

"Oh, Sasha," Helen almost moaned. "Alone?"

The young woman nodded.

"He said I would be rich if I'd go into business with him and," she paused and shook her head like a person waking from a bad dream, "he said if I didn't help, he'd see to it I lost another job."

Martha shivered.

"He and Coraliss must have been the clients in New York who got you fired. Sasha, this means, Reny Redfern may have known who you were for a long time if he requested you by name when you were at Fordham's."

"I know and Louisa, my old director, had an enormous mess to clean up, paid fines, and needed legal representation over being involved with the purchase of the Wytfliet map. Henri was right. It ended up belonging to a small, regional Swedish museum who, as far as I know, has never had it returned to them. Here's the worse part. I think Reny owned R&M Holdings. Why else would they have offered me a job?"

"Not so," Helen countered. "They may have heard of your other successes and wanted to work with you. Don't discount Sir

Alec. If he's your friend, he'll always encourage others to work with you."

Sasha shrugged.

"I hope so. It's been a tough twenty-four hours and I want to wrap up this transaction. I want to be free of this entire situation. We have clearance to go see Mr. McMurray and Mufidy will drive us. He borrowed a car from a greengrocer in Invergarry. I'd like to leave in about thirty minutes."

"We'll be ready," Helen said. "Give us about ten minutes to get back to the boat and collect my satchel."

With a quick two nods, Sasha stood up.

"I'm so sorry for getting you mixed up in this. Thank you for listening."

She turned and walked away and once she was out of earshot, Helen and Martha picked up their heals and followed her, keeping their voices low.

"But it was the steamer, my steamer, they said was the murder weapon," Helen said, her voice rising with hope. "Now it's a windlass?"

With a shrug and a frown, Martha asked, "Could it be both?"

Exchanging quick uncertain expressions, they continued but kept their voices low. Martha weighed her words.

"Why did someone hit Redfern with both the steamer and a windlass?"

"Maybe it wasn't one person," Helen answered.

"That's a possibility," Martha agreed, "but if you wanted to kill Redfern and walked in to see him already dead from a head wound, you wouldn't hit him with a windlass. It's literally overkill."

"Wait," Helen came back. "The steamer had blood on it, but no damaged, remember?"

"True. This business about Matteo's keys going missing is odd, too. If the killer wanted to get rid of Reny, why go to all the trouble of stealing one of the staff's keys to get a windlass? There are plenty of things lying about to whack someone over the head."

"Yes, and it's as if it's a ploy to get the police to look among the guests, not the staff who always would have had access to the deck chest at all times."

Martha nodded. They'd almost reached the boat.

"What is most telling, Helen, is the fact someone left the steamer in your cabin practically beside the body, but out of the blue Mufidy finds a bloody windlass on the opposite end of the boat."

"True," Helen said, her indignation in step with her ascension to the boat's main deck, "but I'd like to say this. Whoever the person is, I have a bone to pick with them. They've killed a man, albeit a terrible man, in my room and wanted to frame me for his murder. Not nice!"

Martha looked over at her affronted but poised friend, and a grin of admiration tugged at the corner of her mouth. Helen was a master of the understated obvious.

"That's right," Martha agreed whole-heartedly, but with a tinge of a tease mixed in, "not nice at all!"

Helen turned and shot her a sour look.

"Okay, okay," Martha said, but her eyes still sparkled. "Let's go to meet the man with the Holinshed, finish with this assessment, and figure out a way to keep you from being arrested. I still think we ought to make a run for it until they find the actual killer."

Throwing up her hands and raising her eyes to the heavens in a gesture of pleading with the Divine, Helen exclaimed, "Bring that up again and I promise to have a proper reason for them to arrest me!"

Chapter Thirty

DCI Moore was as good as her word. The only condition she demanded was they be back and checked in to The Highland Hotel by six o'clock that evening. Mufidy was driving. The van, normally used for groceries, not human transport, had two benches bolted to the inner walls with no cushions, no seat belts, and no heat.

"Is this the only option? It doesn't look safe?" Piers asked Mufidy.

"If they want to go," he grumbled, "this is the only transport available, short of riding horses."

"It'll be fine, Piers," Helen said soothingly. "The drive to Mr. McMurray's home is only about thirty or forty minutes. Hopefully, no dirt roads and the weather's fine. We'll be back for dinner."

She reached up and gave him a consoling kiss on the cheek, eliciting a smile from her worried husband.

"Come here," he said, taking her into his arms. "I love you. Please be careful."

"Helen, I got some fun snacks for the trip!" Martha called as she came out of Invergarry's gas station. "Hope you like cheese puffs, haggis chips, or my favorite, shortbread. I probably won't share the shortbread. Also, I grabbed two cans of something called Irn-Bru."

Watching as a happy Martha clambered into the back of the van with her sack of goodies, Helen turned back around to Piers. Exchanging knowing smiles, they both lightly laughed.

"She adores road trips," Helen said, her tone loving and full of humor. "God only knows what she's got stashed in that bag."

"Well, you've got to give her credit. Her cheese addiction came in handy in Switzerland."

Helen laughed out loud.

"True. Very true."

"Now," Piers said, his tone turning to something more business-like. "I want you to know I've spoken with my solicitor. He's flying up and should be here by tonight. If we're dealing with an eventual arrest, I want as much legal advice as possible."

Taking a deep breath and soaking up the safeness of his arms around her, Helen let out a sigh of gratitude. She looked up into his eyes and smiled.

"Thank you, Piers," she whispered. "Thank you for being so good to me. I love you."

"Are we ready?" Sasha called from the passenger side window. Being the one person who had the directions written on a note-card, they decided she should have the other front seat.

"I'm coming," Helen answered. "Give me a hand."

Helping his wife up into the back, Piers shut the door as the van's engine rumbled into life.

Hunched-over, Helen made her way to her seat and taking out a piece of paper, she laid it on the dirty bench to keep from soiling her clothes. Without luck, she searched for a handle, a strap or anything to hold on to once the van got underway.

"Comfortable?" she asked Martha, who was already munching from a bag of chips.

With a mischievous grin embellished with a couple of chip crumbs, Martha answered, "Use a couple of these. I found them on the floor."

She tossed Helen two long, extremely dirty bungee cords.

"See," Martha said, lifting her purse.

Strapped around her middle were two bungee cords with a third cord going over her shoulder. Martha had then anchored the cords to the van's vertical metal ribs directly behind her.

"If you get them snug enough, it's like a seat belt."

"You've got to be kidding me?" Helen said. "They're covered with gunk."

No sooner were the words out of her mouth than Mufidy hit the gas and the van jolted forward making its insides, outsides, and all things in between shiver, bobble, and rattle with gusto.

"Better get strapped!" Martha yelled over the noise of metal things clanging and the engine's great roaring.

Grabbing the bungee cords from the floor, Helen started strapping herself in. The result resembled something in the Bandito style with two bungee cord bandoliers crisscrossing her chest and hooked to the van's metal ribs.

Martha gave her an appreciative smile and nod.

"That'll work. Are you hungry?" she asked and offered Helen a bag of haggis flavored potato chips.

"Why not," Helen said and accepted the snack half-heartedly.

Tentatively tasting it and finding it unusually tasty, she popped the entire chip into her mouth as Mufidy hit his brakes.

"Hey!" Martha yelled. "We're not a bunch of cabbages back here! Give us some warning before you hit the brakes! I nearly choked on a chip!"

The van skidded to a stop.

"What are we stopping for?" Helen asked.

"It's Mr. Montfort," he called back. "He asked earlier to ride with us up to a hiking area."

Rolling down his window, he talked for a few moments. The van's back door opened.

"Ladies," Edwin Montfort greeted them. "I'm riding with you up to Loch Garry. Thought I'd do some hiking and hopefully on your way back, you'll pick me up."

Both women nodded and smiled.

"Grab a bench," Martha said. "Sorry, we took all the bungee cords, but there's a rope over in the corner. You might use it to tie yourself down."

Helen watched Edwin's gaze fall on the scroungy rope as the greengrocer van lurched forward down the road.

"Thanks, but I'll pass," he said with a chuckle. "Later, if things get too rough."

"Okay," Martha replied. "Better hang on, Edwin. I have a feeling it's going to be a bumpy ride!"

Chapter Thirty-One

"What do you mean Edwin Montfort left?" Moore asked, her voice low and menacing through the phone at her sergeant.

"He's like the others. They went into the village or took walks along the canal path. I'll go collect him if you have other questions, ma'am."

Sergeant McBride was twenty-eight years old and new to his rank. Working with DCI Moore was a never-ending learning curve. She expected him to know what she wanted before she asked.

"Since finding the second murder weapon, Montfort was my next person on the list to ask about the tool chest on deck. Go get him and bring him back," Moore commanded. "Once he's interviewed, transport the guests to the hotel. Keep them there until I have a report back from forensics."

With a quick, "Yes, ma'am," McBride hurried to find Edwin Montfort.

The drive along River Garry up toward Invergarry was one of the many picturesque, romantic roads Scotland had on offer. Wild, unpolluted, and on a day like today, a brooding sense of mystery hung as heavy as the mist over the long glen.

McBride was at home in these pine-covered mountains. Rolling down his side window, he took in a deep breath of the sweet, clean air. It steadied and rejuvenated him. The road curved north with a sprinkling of humans, car, and the usual cyclists always trying their lungs and muscles along the steep hills of the Great Glen.

The village of Invergarry had the regular places visited by tourists. There were restaurants, pubs, and convenience stores, all attracting humans like moths to a streetlight in summer. He headed to the most likely spot, the first oasis of plenty in Invergarry: the gas station.

"Yes, a group left here in the larder's van," a woman, the manager, told McBride. "The man driving works on The Caledonian Queen. He's a handsome devil, about fifty named Lewis Mufidy. I didn't know the women, so they must have been guests from the boat."

"You didn't see another man come through here who's about the same age as Lewis Mufidy, but an American, tall but with dark brown hair?" McBride asked her.

She pursed her mouth in concentration and rolled the pucker to the left along with her eyes out to the road that ran in front of the filling station.

"This time of year we see so many hikers and tourists coming through, it's impossible to remember them all. You might ask in the village. We have a cafe and a community building with public toilets. The people who work there may remember."

McBride's mobile phone rang. It was DCI Moore.

"Find him?" she snapped.

"No, ma'am, but I will."

"Take only another hour to look for him. We've got bigger problems."

McBride's stomach muscles constricted. He swallowed hard before asking, "Here, ma'am? May I ask why?"

"The father-in-law of Reny Redfern, a Senator Anderson, is flying into an airport near Inverness. He wants to know where his daughter, Coraliss Redfern, is whose phone went off-line two days ago. Here's the fun part. He's bringing his own FBI investigation team who've traced her phone's last signal to our jurisdiction, but somewhere up in the mountains. We've probably got some sort of international situation on our hands, McBride. We've got to have the murder investigation tied up fast."

"Yes, ma'am," was all McBride squeezed in.

"I want all the guests rounded up and back on this boat in the next few hours. Find Montfort, find that Cousins woman, and Sasha Pelletier. Mobile phones won't work further inland, so you're on your own. They were to meet a Mr. Arthur McMurray who lives near Tomchrasky."

Sergeant McBride's stomach dropped like a bowling ball. Finding people up in the mountains was always a challenge.

"I'll bring them in, Ma'am."

He ended the call and said goodbye to the store manager. Two bikers down the road remembered seeing the greengrocer van stopping and picking up a man. They pointed along the A87 road which would fork near the River Moriston toward Tomchrasky.

McBride thanked them, rolled up his window, and stepped on the gas.

Chapter Thirty-Two

A delicate mist filtered and blessed every pebble, every wind-swept blade of grass and in its impartiality, the battered greengrocer van. Through one of many rusted out cracks, a tiny leak trickled into the van's interior only inches away from where Martha sat on her rock-hard bench. The tiny rivulet meandered along its course to its first stopping point in a puddle directly below her seat. The wet, the cold, and the discomfort were breeding a slow-growing irritation in Martha. She shut her eyes and tried to think of happy thoughts. Donuts sprang to mind first.

Back and forth the wipers beat out a rhythm. Intermittently, they screeched out a whine telling all who depended on them how worn they were from their long-suffering service. Those on the bench seats were in agreement with the wipers. Bottoms were bruising, and backs were aching. The smell of a forgotten cabbage hiding somewhere under a pile of wet sacks in the corner saturated the confines of their space, resulting in a rancid, noxious odor for all to breathe.

"How far do we have before we're there?" Helen called up to the front, her face a shade of grey.

Sasha sighed and shook her head.

"I have no reception here. My map application doesn't show the address for Mr. McMurray's house and these directions he gave me are hard to follow. I think once we get to Tomchrasky, we will have to stop and ask for directions. Shouldn't be another ten minutes."

Worry tinged her last few words.

"Good," Martha grumbled and rubbed her hip. "I call dibs on the passenger seat for the ride home, Sasha!"

"Are you sure you want out in this weather?" Helen asked Edwin. "You didn't exactly dress for it and it'll be even cooler the further up into the mountains we go."

Edwin Montfort shot a quick look out the back window of the van and sighed.

"I left my good rain jacket thinking it would be fine. I didn't foresee the weather when I left the boat. Not exactly smart of me," he answered. "I'll tag along and wait in the van if you don't mind."

"If we can't find it, how in the world will Sir Alec make it here today?" Martha asked. "Have you spoken to him, Sasha?"

Turning around with some difficulty from her seatbelt, Sasha called back to the third-class seats.

"He came up last night and stayed in Fort Augustus. I spoke with him before we left the boat and explained we wouldn't be riding together. He will use the driver I arranged. I'm sure they'll find it okay."

"We should ride home with Sir Alec and have the driver take us to the hotel," Martha said. "I don't want to be a whiner, Mufidy, but I don't think my back end will survive a return trip."

"More than fine by me," the morose Mufidy replied. "If you want to use the other car to take you to the hotel, I'll drop you off and head back to Invergarry. I've plenty to do."

Martha and Helen exchanged expressions, meaning Mufidy was testy. He'd not spoken the entire trip except for a few yeses and nos. His only other full sentence was back at the gas station, making it clear he preferred Matteo, the steward, to have done this errand.

Though the A87 was an excellently paved road, the van's worn-out suspension and transmission had seen better days. The bouncing reduced Helen to using an old blanket to buffer her bottom while Martha sat on top of her jacket and two rolls of paper towels. Edwin never complained although Martha noticed he winced once or twice when Mufidy hit the brakes hard.

Feeling irritable and also bored, Martha lowered her gaze upon Edwin Montfort. He sat upon the opposite bench alongside Helen, looking out the back window and occasionally stealing glances at Helen's nice legs. People fascinated Martha. It was time to learn more about Edwin. Best to take the direct approach, she thought.

"So, what's your alibi for Reny Redfern's time of death?"

The question brought the man's head up with a snap, his face registering an expression of surprise. Helen's eyes twinkled with humor, but she didn't smile.

"I...well...I told the inspector I was probably in my room when he was killed," he said. "What's *your* alibi?"

Martha shrugged and sighed.

"Don't have one, and if you think about it, Edwin, none of us do."

"Well, I do," Edwin returned defiantly.

Martha offered him a crooked, curious smile.

"Do tell," she said encouragingly.

Edwin's chin jutted forward and his eyebrows raised as if he was considering the time frame.

"As I said, I was asleep in my cabin."

"Sure," Martha replied, "but what if someone killed Reny Redfern in the morning, not at night like the police want to believe? What would happen to your alibi then, Edwin?"

Chapter Thirty-Three

❧❧❧

"That's her!" Lucy McCreedie cried pointing to the tv screen hanging at the end of the pub's bar. "That's the woman I saw pushed off the cliff!"

As the words flew from her mouth, they brought everyone standing around her to focus their attention on the television and the news announcement about an American senator whose daughter was missing.

A good majority of the dart competitors, finished with the Edinburgh Darts Invitational, were in The Grog Soaked Admiral partaking of either a drink of good cheer or one of good sport. Either way, it was a merry crowd, and standing at the end of the bar was Johns waiting on his refill and the photographer to call his team over to take their photo. The exclamation made by the delicate-looking young woman at the end of the bar made him turn to look at the screen.

"Senator Anderson will arrive this afternoon by private jet to meet with law enforcement officials. According to an insider source, the senator will liaise with Federal Bureau of Investigation agents and Police Scotland officers to search for his daughter, Coraliss Redfern, whose last known mobile location was near Grantown-On-Spey in the Abernethy National Nature Reserve.

Mrs. Redfern, the wife of billionaire, Reny Redfern, was last seen at a charity event in Yorkshire."

Johns slowly shook his head from side to side as a picture of Senator Anderson with his daughter Coraliss exchanged places with one of Reny Redfern.

"They don't know he's dead," Johns muttered to himself.

He'd no sooner made the mental decision to make a call to Police Scotland's office in Fort Augustus than the woman made another announcement.

"That's the man I saw!" she blurted. "That's the man who pushed her!"

The other patrons, indifferent to the woman's exclamations, went about the business of celebration. Johns, however, grabbed his beer and went down to the end of the bar where she stood riveted to the spot under the television.

"Excuse me," he said as he wormed his way in between her and a corpulent man with a bright red shirt emblazoned with 'Cock and Bottle' across the back. "Did you say you recognized both people?" he asked her.

Lucy McCreedie turned around. Her owlish eyes scanned his face. Cocking her head to one side, she considered him with unblinking steadiness.

"I do. The man," she thumbed in the television's direction, "killed the woman. I'm going straight to the police. Who are you?"

"I'm with the police in Yorkshire. My team is up here for the tournament."

Johns pulled out his badge and identification, laying it on the bar for Lucy to inspect. Taking out her cell phone, she looked back at him, her face devoid of emotion.

"Do you mind?" she asked, indicating she wished to snap a photo of his identification.

"That's fine," he answered with a nod.

After giving the ID a thorough going over, she handed it back to him and offered her hand for him to shake.

"I'm Lucy McCreedie," she said. "I was there the day this

Redfern person pushed his wife over the cliff. The Crested Tit, a rare but exceptional bird, was my objective that day. I was scanning an area when my binoculars rested on two people standing on an outcropping. It happened before I realized what I was seeing."

She stopped and took a drink from her glass of beer. Johns waited quietly. People retell events, especially horrible ones, better if they're left to feel their way slowly through the wreckage.

"The man walked up with a smile on his face. He pushed her. She had his back to him. I saw the surprise on her face as she fell. He looked over the edge of the cliff, nothing on his face. His lips moved like he was saying something, then he walked away."

Her words died to a whisper, barely audible over the din of jovial Grog Soaked Admiral patrons. In her glazed eyes, Johns saw the reflection of what she'd witnessed. They stood like two odd trees, unmoving and untouched by the loud wind of humanity whipping around them, a wild dance of whirling characters and fleeting tastes.

"I'm sorry for what you saw," Johns offered after a long pause.

Lucy nodded and swallowed the last sip of her beer.

"We, the rangers and I, found her after following a trail up to a spot where the pines left off growing. They broke her fall."

For a moment neither spoke, then Johns' thoughts returned to Martha, Helen and Piers.

"I have friends near Fort Augustus who knew Coraliss and Reny Redfern. How certain are you about it being Redfern who pushed this woman?"

The owl eyes blinked and rounded, into even larger, dark pools of unreadability. A twitch of her tightly compressed mouth hinted there was much mental cogitation taking place to compose her answer. She nodded up and down.

"I'll never forget that face. I know he deliberately killed her. It's him all right."

Johns' mouth set into a hard line. He shifted his gaze down to his untried pint as if the answer for men's malice was floating among the Bitter's bubbles.

"I'm going to Fort Augustus. The police need to know you recognized Reny Redfern as Coraliss' murderer," he said, his tone flat, unquestionable.

Lucy screwed up her mouth in a tight pucker and rolled it to one side of her round, pale face. The rowdy dart players laughed and carried on around them reminding Johns there was laughter and tears, kindness and cruelty, hope and fear in any moment of existence.

Lucy appeared to know her mind.

"Would you take me along? I'll follow in my car."

Johns nodded, his focus still on the pint in front of him. It hit him. Perigrine had driven them to Edinburgh.

"I don't have a car. I drove up here with friends."

Leaning backward, she gave him a hard, calculated look.

"I guess we could ride together," she said. "I'd need to take a picture of your badge and make a few calls."

Johns, his manner slow and unperturbed, laughed good-naturedly.

"Good safety precautions but let me do you one better."

"Okay."

Johns took one napkin from the bar and wrote on it. Pulling his badge from his pocket, he handed it to her again.

"Here's my badge, here's the number to the Marsden-Lacey Constabulary where I'm the DCI, and here is my superintendent's phone number. Take pictures of all three and send them to your mum or whoever. Give my superintendent a call."

Lucy shot him a smile.

"Good," she said. "When can we leave?"

Chapter Thirty-Four

❧❧❧

Martha watched Helen shift uncomfortably on the van's bench. Their conversation was veering a touch too close to Helen's earlier revelation about Reny.

With the trip up to Mr. McMurray's having turned into more of a scenic ramble than a direct route, she'd had time to wiggle around in the last twenty-four hours and try to remember the comings and goings of the passengers on The Caledonian Queen. What she needed was a way to prove Reny was alive after Helen returned to the breakfast table that morning.

Only the killer would be privy to the exact time of Reny's death, but Martha was hoping Edwin might have seen or heard something that would help Helen's case. It wouldn't hurt to dig into his memory a bit. They had plenty of time.

She watched Edwin's reaction. His eyebrows knitted together and his jaw muscle twitched.

"What would make you think they killed him in the morning when the police believe differently?" he snipped.

Shifting his weight, his mouth in a hard line, he appeared to wait for her response.

Martha held up her finger and wagged it back and forth.

"Well, ya see, Edwin, I remember putting in the cabin's closet a bottle of champagne and a bag of chips I may have purloined yesterday from the bar. I did this before I knew Piers, Helen's husband, would kick me from my bed."

A suffering sigh came from Helen's direction. Martha chose not to make eye contact with her annoyed friend but pushed on with her deductions.

"I was trying to hide the...treats, shall we say, from Matteo. Helen and Piers retrieved the bottle of champagne when they went up to the deck for a romantic stroll around ten o'clock, but they left the bag of chips. It's the chips, Edwin. You must pay attention to the chip trail. They are the key to this thing."

She flashed Edwin a brilliant grin. He countered with a bored expression and hooded eyes.

"That's right!" Helen exclaimed, coming out of her martyrdom momentarily. "I don't remember seeing the bag of chips when we found Reny this morning..."

There was a distinct deceleration in Helen's speech as if an unsavory truth was sneaking up on her.

"Hey! Wait a minute!" she blurted. "The closet where we found the champagne was MY closet, not yours!"

Martha nodded, her eyes round with meaning.

"That's right. Thank you for finally admitting that. You're beginning to see."

"I'm beginning to see you were hiding your ill-gotten booty in MY closet!"

A quick deflection was in order.

"You're missing the point, Helen," Martha said, trying to sound soothing. "When I stashed the stuff, I thought we would hang out, drink champagne, eat chips, watch a movie. You know, girl-night stuff."

Helen's tightly pursed mouth indicated she wasn't ready to drop the bone of irritation yet, but Martha plowed onward.

"When I went back into the cabin this morning it was to

retrieve the chips. I knew Matteo would come in later to straighten the rooms and I didn't want him to find them. I lifted them from the bar, and he'd know in an instant it wasn't Helen who'd stolen them. She's more of a Brie on an apple wedge kind of girl."

Edwin shrugged, spread his hands, and laid them upon his knees.

"So? That doesn't mean someone killed him during the morning."

"But, Edwin," Martha replied sounding like a patient school-marm, "I snuck into Helen and Piers' cabin around two o'clock in the morning to retrieve those chips."

"You came into our room?" Helen interjected. "While we were sleeping? We *were* sleeping? Tell me right now we were asleep?" Helen demanded, her words revealing her discombobulated under-standing of Martha's operating system.

"Well, uh, I guess," Martha answered, drawing out the last word. "But I couldn't retrieve the chips at that moment." Turning back to Edwin and ignoring Helen's clenched jaw and flame-throwing glare, she added, "This is the important part. When I left the cabin, I locked the door making it impossible for anyone to stuff Reny in the closet until after Helen and Piers went to breakfast."

"I disagree," Edwin said with a flat expression.

Helen and Martha gave him a vinegary look.

"Well, not to put too fine a point on it but," he thumbed in Helen's direction and pointed at Martha, "one of you did it or her husband. Who else had better access to the cabin than all of you?"

"And stuff him in their own closet!" Martha snapped. "Only an idiot would stuff a corpse in their own closet, Edwin."

"Or someone very smart," he snapped back.

Martha gave a huff, but before she responded, Helen jumped into the fray.

"WE DID NOT KILL ANYONE!" Helen declared adamantly.

"As for your assumption, Mr. Montfort, why in the world, if you believed we are hardened murderers, would you get into this van with us?"

Relieved Edwin had unwittingly tossed himself in front of Helen like a sacrificial lamb, Martha stayed mute. Helen needed an outlet after learning about Martha's nighttime scavenging habits. Edwin's face spoke volumes in its bewilderment, his mouth open, but no words issuing from it.

"Well?" Helen demanded, her eyebrows raised tauntingly, and her back rigid with indignation. "Nothing? Fine! Let me tell you something," she said. "Someone dumped Reny Redfern in my cabin and to be perfectly candid with you, Mr. Montfort, I'm extremely offended by their obvious lack of decency. If I wanted to get rid of a body, I wouldn't pawn it off on some poor unsuspecting innocent. I'd do the right thing and dispose of it properly myself."

With her reprimand spent, Helen gave a harrumph and settled herself, arms crossed, and back against the van's inner wall. Martha noted she'd flashed her an icy look as well.

Edwin Montfort looked back and forth between the two women with the gaze of a wary rabbit.

"I wouldn't be in this van if I thought you were the murderer, Mrs. Cousins. I was playing devil's advocate by merely pointing out any of *you* could have done it."

Martha and Helen shrugged at the same time.

"Point taken, Edwin," Martha conceded, feeling bad for him. After all, he'd been the accidental dupe for Helen's wrath. "We didn't kill Reny. The bag of chips I went back for this morning was gone. Gone! Do you see?"

Both Edwin and Helen stared at her.

"Someone in between the time I locked the door, and I came back in after Helen and Piers went to breakfast stole those chips. They weren't there when I went to retrieve them this morning and found Reny's body."

"And we never saw them when we took the champagne from

the closet," Helen added, sounding less miffed. "Did you see them when you came into our room last night?"

Nodding her head, Martha said, "Oh yes, I saw them. I'd hidden them under some of your stuff, but, well, you kinda moved in the bed, and Piers was shifting about. I was afraid if I'd grabbed the bag it might make a crinkle sound. So just as my hand was hovering over the chip bag, I decided to leave."

Helen's mouth dropped, and her nostrils flared. Martha wasn't exactly sure, but steam may have been wafting from her friend's ears. The greengrocer van had become a hotbed of trust and personal boundary issues.

Before Martha explained further, the van tossed its contents around like popcorn kernels on a hot cast iron pan. It threw all three bench wranglers about, making them grapple for anything that offered a handhold for stability.

"What's going on?" Martha called loudly over the racket from things clanking, banging and thumping.

"We've taken a dirt road which we hope is the direction to Mr. McMurray's house," Sasha yelled back. "I'm so sorry but Mufidy believes this might be the right way. Hang on and we should see something soon."

Mufidy had a special way of driving over the Highland dirt roads. He aimed the van at the biggest rocks in the road, ran over them, catapulting the vehicle over a dozen lesser obstacles. If the van survived, it would only do so by breaking down and forcing Mufidy to walk back to Invergarry.

Martha knew the look on Helen's face. There was a widening fissure of wrath about to unleash a molten blast of rage upon the driver of the greengrocer van. The impending eruption filled her own heart with sweet, warm pleasure. Helen was a lady to the last thread of her perfectly chosen tailored suit, but there was only so much she would swallow with grace.

"Mufidy!" Helen bellowed from her seat, one hand with a death grip on the edge of the bench and the other tight-fisted around a swinging bungee cord strapped to the van's rib cage. "Stop this van at once! I've had enough!"

The van came to an abrupt, shuddering stop.

Martha could have kissed Helen for issuing her command, saving them from shaken-brain syndrome, but for one thing. Edwin had a gun, and it was pointing in her direction.

Chapter Thirty-Five

"Senator Anderson will arrive in about an hour at the Royal Air Force station in Moray. We've received a call from a park ranger working in The Abernethy National Nature Reserve who saw the news today regarding the senator's visit to find his lost daughter. She says the woman they found a few days ago meets the description of Coraliss Redfern. The body is in a hospital morgue at Inverness as an unidentified female. The park ranger left her number for you."

DCI Moore's tense muscles in her neck relaxed as the dispatcher related his information. That's what this job did to you. It made you grateful they found a body. She shook her head at the perverseness of her job.

"Thank you, sergeant, I'll drive up and meet Senator Anderson."

A buzz of delight warmed Moore's usually reticent heart. Raising her eyes heavenward, she sought some edification from the divine for its unusually swift response to a prayer not even asked... yet. What was happening here? In the flash of an eye, a simple two-minute telephone call had solved a nasty problem.

A tired, thankful, and bewildered smile crept across her ordinarily hard line of a mouth. The job shaped an officer into a cynical creature, which accounted for the progression of her following thoughts. There had to be a catch.

"One thing more, ma'am," the dispatcher came back, "I've had a call from a detective chief inspector with the Marsden-Lacey Constabulary in Yorkshire. He asked to speak with the inspector in charge of the Redfern case."

"Odd," she mused into the phone. "Wonder what he wants?"

"He didn't go into detail, ma'am, but wanted to speak directly."

A tiny inkling of tension brewed again in her recently relaxed neck muscle.

"What's his name, this inspector from Yorkshire?" she asked, her words sounding wary.

"DCI Merriam Johns."

Moore nodded sagely. There it was and so neatly tied up with a fat, red bow. Fate or whatever it was running the show up there had a lovely sense of humor. She sighed.

Keeping the politicians happy whether they be Scottish higher-ups in her command or American diplomats who expected police reinforcement was part of her job. She meant to do it to the best of her abilities, even when it meant working with an old rival like Johns.

"I know the man," her tone dry. "Give him my number, sergeant. I'd like to know what he knows since he's in a sharing mood. Also, text me the number of the ranger from Abernethy. I want to call her."

The day was tumbling into early afternoon, and with it, the weather had shifted. Low clouds full of mist were rolling off into the East and patches of sunshine cheered the skies. Having finished with the dispatcher, Moore took a cue from the weather and looked on these benefices as good things.

On the plus sheet, she counted two points in her favor. There was a possible body to show Anderson and forensics confirmed the windlass was the weapon used to kill Reny Redfern. All she needed was Sergeant McBride to find the four gadabouts who'd rambled off to some unknown antiquary's cottage and bring them back here. McBride was good at his job. He'd find them.

As for now, if she was to receive the call from Johns, it would be better to have any loose ends tied down about the death of Redferns, one and two. Getting a call into the ranger in Abernethy was a priority. Moore wanted to have as much information about Coraliss Redfern's death as possible. Receiving help from Johns, once he knew who she was, might dry up fast.

Twenty years ago, they'd worked together as fresh recruits in Leeds. They'd clashed. She'd been intent on moving up through the ranks as much as he, but he received promotions at a faster rate. Moore didn't blame it on being a woman. She blamed it on Johns' inability to be a team player. The last thing she remembered about him was he'd gone off to accept a detective inspector's position somewhere. His leaving gave her some room to stretch.

Dialing the number, the dispatcher sent over, Moore walked to her car. To meet Senator Anderson, she needed to leave now. Hopefully, the ranger would be in the office.

"Abernethy National Nature Reserve Ranger Station, Harriet Darrow speaking."

"Hello, my name is DCI Verity Moore with the Fort Augustus Police. I'm acting officer in charge of the Coraliss Redfern missing person case. My dispatcher rang me with your information about finding a woman who'd died falling from a cliff in the reserve. Would you be able to tell me more about what you know? The photos of Coraliss Redfern put up by the news media, do they resemble the woman you found?"

"Yes, I believe it is her, but can't be certain. We received a call from a terrified woman who'd been out birdwatching a few days ago. She claimed to have seen with her binoculars a woman pushed from an outcropping. Hysterical, she was."

"What was this woman's name?" Moore asked.

"Lucy McCreedie. Lives in Edinburgh. She'd found a cellular reception point up a few kilometers from Grantown-On-Spey and called us. We met her and she showed us approximately where she saw the woman fall. Took us four hours to trek back into the area, but she was right. We found the body."

"Do you have any reason to believe she may have had anything to do with Coraliss Redfern's fall?"

There was a momentary silence before the ranger replied.

"No, I don't. Ms. McCreedie was extremely upset and she was determined to go with us to retrieve the woman's body. We worked with the Inverness police for over five hours out there and Ms. McCreedie wouldn't leave. We put her up in a hotel that evening because we worried about her driving back to Edinburgh alone."

"Do you have McCreedie's number?"

"Yes, ma'am."

"If you would, please text it to me. Thank you for your help."

Moore finished her call and turned the ignition over, pulling free from the car park where she'd left her vehicle. Basking in the sunlight pouring down through the windscreen, she smiled like a content cat who'd found a warm, windless corner of a summer garden.

The text message from Harriet Darrow would arrive soon, and in an hour she would be meeting with Senator Anderson. It wouldn't be a pleasant job to tell the father his daughter was dead, but better to have a concrete answer to give him than to spend the next few weeks struggling to find a missing person, especially one with such strong diplomatic obligations.

Like all timing in nature, the text arrived exactly at the same moment as her car's internal phone connection announced an incoming call. Ignoring the text, she tapped the answer button on the dash screen.

"DCI Moore."

"Hello," came a man's voice.

She recognized it instantly.

"Would this be DCI *Verity* Moore?"

Did she detect a twinge of incredulity in the man's voice? Her mouth pulled up into a distasteful pucker. Better to play it off like a pure professional.

"Yes, this is DCI Verity Moore of the Fort Augustus Police. How may I help you?"

Her tone hopefully indicated her extreme lack of time due to a busy, critical caseload.

"This is DCI Merriam Johns. How are you, Verity? Long time since we were recruits together. I know how busy you are at the moment, but I may have some information to help with the Coraliss Redfern situation."

She didn't hesitate in her quick response. Anything less would look like a sour grapes situation.

"How are you, Merriam? I would appreciate any information you may offer."

"I've been in Edinburgh, but I'm coming to Fort Augustus. I have friends on the hotel barge where there's been a murder. You're the investigating officer for the murder of Reny Redfern on The Caledonian Queen, correct? Your sergeant working dispatch wasn't at liberty to give information."

That pesky neck muscle of hers relapsed into an impression of a pilates bungee strap. Friends? Who were his *friends*? Was he coming up to insert himself in her investigation? Probably, and if he did, he'd be in for a surprise. This wasn't his jurisdiction.

"Who are your friends, Johns?" she asked.

"Piers and Helen Cousins."

The bungee muscle nearly snapped.

"Helen Cousins," she said with slow deliberation. "Have you been on the phone with either of them? This is my investigation, Johns. If you have any information regarding this case, you must turn it over to me. You know that."

It was a death-like silence that came back to her. When he responded, she heard the coolness in his tone.

"I do. I have spoken with Piers. He called for advice. That's not the reason I'm coming to Fort Augustus. I've been at a darts tournament in Edinburgh and call it Fate or pure coincidence, but I happen to be standing in a pub when the photos of Coraliss Redfern came over the news."

DCI Moore stayed mute until it was necessary to say something to encourage his continuance.

"I met the woman who says she knows who killed Coraliss Redfern."

Moore didn't miss a beat.

"You met Lucy McCreedie," she stated.

"I did. She recognized Coraliss Redfern, and she recognized the killer. I told her I was going to Fort Augustus. Ms. McCreedie wanted to come. I'm bringing her. Where do you want to meet her?"

"Who does she think killed Coraliss Redfern?" Moore asked, ignoring his question.

Johns' reply was succinct, ignoring her question in return.

"She wants to see the body."

Moore squinted her eyes, annoyed but also trying to catch his meaning.

"Body? She's already seen Coraliss Redfern's body."

"Not Coraliss' body, Verity. Lucy McCreedie wants to see the body of the man who she believes killed Coraliss Redfern. She wants to see *Reny Redfern*."

Chapter Thirty-Six

"**S**top the van!" Edwin yelled up to the front.

"What for?" Mufidy called over his shoulder. "We stop now, and I might not get this box of bolts ever going again."

All of her peevish feelings toward Martha bled from Helen's mind the minute she realized Edwin had pulled the gun from his thin windbreaker and pointed it at her dearest friend.

"Hey!" she said to him, her own words sounding hollow to her. "What are you doing?"

In her mind, she struggled with why mild-mannered Edwin was wielding a gun. Was he angry because she yelled at him or afraid because he thought they were murderers?

"Shut up!" he barked at her, his face dark and without the earlier aspect of affability. "I want this van stopped right now!"

Getting up from the bench, Edwin struggled to maintain his equilibrium with the van's bumping about on the goat path-of-a-road. He wobbled up to the front.

Swinging her gaze toward Martha, who was stealthily trying to undo her bungee cord seat belts, Helen pointed her toe and nudged Martha's foot trying to catch her attention.

Martha looked up at her and mouthed, "Get your cords off. Hurry."

Giving a quick nod, Helen worked the cords, wrapped around her chest and waist. Trembling fingers made the job go slower than her mind found acceptable.

"Stupid cords," she muttered.

Edwin continued his slow progress, finally making it to the front of the van. Though it was going at a snail's speed already, Mufidy's box of bolts came to an even deader stop when Edwin cold-cocked the grumpy driver over the head, sending Mufidy's entire upper body forward until it hung like a wet rag over the steering wheel.

Sasha, who'd turned at the cracking sound of the gun smashing against Mufidy's skull, screamed, her face melting into an expression of horror as she saw the gun in Edwin's hand. Reeling backward away from Edwin as someone stung from a vicious wasp, Sasha pulled the door handle and fell from the passenger seat, hitting the ground beside the van.

A surge of rage rushed through Helen at Edwin's cruelty. Her hands tore at one cord, sending it hurtling through the air and nearly missing Martha's face. It came to rest like a bizarre, weirdly placed earring caught in Martha's curly red hair.

Both friends looked at each other like surprised guinea fowl birds.

"What are you doing?" Martha hissed, but Edwin cut Helen off from answering.

"Get out!" he demanded, waving the firearm at them.

Bungeed as they were with multiple straps crisscrossing their chests and torsos, they stared dumbly at him. From where Sasha fell, a whimpering sound caught Helen's attention, as well as Edwin's. Helen watched him turn and study something on the ground. He lowered the pistol, his expression cold.

Like she was in a vacuum, all sound ceased except for blood rushing through her eardrums. Her voice cut through the silence.

"My God! What are you doing?"

Edwin turned to look at her, his arm still extended away from his body with the gun's barrel pointed down at its victim.

"Not what *I'm* doing, Mrs. Cousins, but what the police will believe *you've* done."

Chapter Thirty-Seven

The airport marshaller's hand signals guided the white charter jet to a stopping spot on the tarmac. DCI Moore watched as an efficient military crew, fighting against strong, rain-drenched gusts of wind, hurried to position the passenger ramp at the aircraft's main side door.

Above the action taking place upon the ground, flew a pair of black crows. Circling once, they came to settle upon the jet's unspoiled, glossy roof. DCI Moore, distracted for a moment by the bird's cawing, wing flapping, and strutting along their sleek, metal cousin's back, didn't immediately notice the cabin door swinging open.

Senator Anderson stepped onto the short platform and descended the stairs. A coterie of men dressed in either blue or black suits and with mainly red or yellow ties cinched about their necks followed him.

"Not a woman in the bunch," the female detective muttered to herself. "This should be interesting."

DCI Moore waited for the suits to enter the unadorned and basic military airport's waiting room. Two customs agents asked the men questions and scanned their luggage, briefcases, and other personal bags. Once they'd finished, Moore approached the senator with her identification held so he would easily see her credentials.

"Senator Anderson," she greeted him, her tone professional, but pleasant. "I'm DCI Verity Moore. I'm the officer in charge of your daughter's case. Would you have a moment to talk privately?"

After a quick appraisal of her person, she caught the fleeting hint of dislike in the good senator's expression. Years of reading people gave Moore an advantage in sussing out people's deeper, truer nature.

Anderson, blue-eyed with his generic blond hair cut and styled in the typical conservative American politician way, stood over six feet tall. He looked the quintessentially successful man, but Moore caught the whiff of ruthlessness tinged with cruelty clinging to him like an acrid cologne.

He took a deep breath and released it through his nostrils like a frustrated horse. Looking down at her, he replied to her question with a question, his tone depreciatory.

"Are you the welcoming committee?"

"Sir?" she responded, uncertain of his meaning.

"No press?" he asked looking past her into the parking lot beyond.

Verity Moore did the math. Two years ago she'd traveled to New York on vacation. The US elections were in full swing at the time. So, since America staggered its senatorial elections every two years, it must be time for another round of stumping for votes.

Moore, jaded from years working homicide investigations, wondered if Anderson was using his daughter's disappearance to get voter sympathy and media coverage. She didn't bother to scan the parking lot behind her. The media, if they showed at all, would go to Inverness and Fort Augustus, that is, if something more titil-lating or devastating wasn't happening elsewhere in the world.

"Senator Anderson, I'd like to fill you in on what we've learned so far regarding your daughter, Coraliss Redfern. If you would, please, I think we should talk in private. I've arranged a van for your convenience to take you to Inverness."

"I'm heading inland to Grantown-on-Spey," he said. "That was my daughter's last known location."

One of the junior men standing behind Anderson cut free from the herd and stepped forward.

"Officer Moore," he said, his tone respectful, "I'm Special Agent Quinn. What information do you have to share about Mrs. Redfern?"

Moore hadn't wanted to divulge the report about Coraliss' body being found in such an abrupt manner, but it must be done.

"I think we should sit down," she said, first addressing Senator Anderson and shifting her gaze to Agent Quinn.

Anderson's eyebrows shot up and his jaw slackened.

"Sir, there is seating over here," Moore said and walked toward a few chairs lined-up along the waiting room's dingy wall.

Once seated, the men turned to her with faces devoid of emotion.

"Senator Anderson, a woman's body meeting the description of your daughter was found a few days ago in a rocky ravine in Abernethy National Nature Reserve close to Grantown-On-Spey. We need someone to identify the body. It's in a hospital morgue in Inverness." Moore took a deep breath and added, "I'm also sorry to say, sir, her husband, Reny Redfern, was murdered this morning on a hotel barge near Invergarry."

Anderson sat not moving. Did she catch a slight relaxation of the muscles around his eyes? His hand trembled as he raised it to his brow and rubbed one of the fine creases etched there.

"I guess we'd better go to the morgue," he said, his voice hoarse. "I didn't expect this...I thought she was merely upset and her threats..."

His words trailed off, but Moore grabbed at their frayed ends and asked, "Threats? Did your daughter threaten something?"

In her mind, Moore wondered if Lucy McCreedie saw a murder *or* if she saw a suicide.

Anderson's head wobbled upward until his gaze connected with hers. His focus narrowed slowly until he answered, "She often when she wanted something, would go somewhere and not answer her phone." Anderson took a breath and finished. "Coraliss wasn't happy with Reny or even me lately. We'd butted heads, and she'd threatened to — leave."

Anderson dropped his head once again, his open palms lying upturned in his lap.

"I need to see this body. I need to know for sure if it's Coraliss."

DCI Moore, her mouth compressed in a hard line, looked up at Special Agent Quinn. Without words, her expression conveyed it wasn't a question of *if* it was Coraliss Redfern.

Quinn took the hint and took charge.

"Senator, if you'll come with us, we should be in Inverness in less than twenty minutes."

Like a man in a trance, he stood up, letting Quinn steer him toward the waiting van. No one spoke. It was as if cold, unapologetic reality had replaced Anderson hope.

For Verity Moore though, her years as a detective had ingrained in her a sixth sense for when something smelled wrong. Senator Anderson's answer about his daughter's threats and his almost negligible facial response to the news about his son-in-law's murder didn't ring true. She'd bet a month's pay Anderson was worried about something else.

As they pulled out of the parking lot, Moore looked out through her rain-smeared window. Waiting patiently on the tarmac, where it stopped only minutes ago, was the man-made aviation marvel used to whisk a powerful man thousands of miles in comfort and elegance. A murder of crows capered upon its metal back, now covered with an agglomeration of repugnant bird droppings. Hopping, squawking and pecking at the winged creature, they implied their disfavor with the phony bird's deception.

"They're so intelligent," Moore thought to herself. "Even they know a fraud when they see one."

Chapter Thirty-Eight

❧✦☙

"I killed her?" Helen exclaimed. "Why in the world would you want to hurt Sasha and blame *me* for it?"

Edwin Montfort, standing upright with his pistol, lowered the firearm's barrel at Sasha. The question incited a chuckle from him, followed by a surprising answer.

"I don't give a damn about Sasha Pelletier except for the fact she's brokering a deal for me. She's got the same blood in her veins as that bastard, Redfern. For that reason alone, we should remove her from the gene pool of humanity."

Keeping him talking meant he wouldn't pull the trigger. Martha jumped in with Martha's direct style.

"Did you kill Reny Redfern, Edwin?"

The pistol hand noticeably drooped. He shook his head left to right and laughed, his tone rueful.

"It was the chips. I can't believe a damn bag of barbecue chips tripped me up."

Finally disentangled from her cords, Martha sighed.

"One way or another, chips catch up with a person, Edwin. I know." She looked down at her modest pooch-of-a-belly and took a deep breath, pushing on. "Did you take the chips *after* you killed Reny?"

The muscles around his eyes tightened as Edwin's gaze rested on Martha's face. The gun arm sagged a few more inches.

"I took them because I had to get rid of them. Reny was sitting on the edge of the bed eating them," he replied, his words coming slowly and his eyes glazing as if he was relating a dream. "He'd been rifling through the closet, probably looking for information about the manuscript Helen would be assessing. I overheard your heated argument, too, Helen. When you left, I popped in for a talk with Reny. He asked me what I was doing on the boat and told me he knew about R&M Holdings. Of course, he wanted the manuscript. He'd figured it out, so I told him, if he wanted the manuscript, he'd have to admit his criminality in the oil tanker's wreck along Scotland's north coast. He'd have to make reparations."

"Manuscript?" Martha interjected. "Do you mean the Holinshed?"

Her question didn't register with him. He kept to his storyline.

"Reny stood up and shoved the bag at me. In his usual smug-bastard way, he told me to shove my pathetic dream of blackmailing him and he would get the manuscript without my help. The chips fell all over me and the red seasoning stained my shirt."

A sereneness stole across Edwin's face.

"That's when I hit him over the head."

No one dared to speak. Unmoving, his eyes clouded with a memory.

Helen asked, "Exactly what manuscript are we talking about? The Holinshed?"

Behind Edwin, she saw Sasha's hand grip the edge of the van's door frame. With her entire mental focus, Helen tried to send her a silent warning to stay quiet and seek a hiding place. Turning, Edwin looked at Helen as if he'd forgotten Sasha all together.

"It was Reny's fault the tanker went down," he said. "I co-owned the company with him that built the navigational software, but Reny also sat on the multinational bank's board who financed the tanker manufacturing company based out of New Orleans.

Reny forced the implementation of the navigational software before it was ready. He liked to cross-pollinate, as he put it, which meant using companies he owned to buy or use products from other companies for which he sat on boards. Once it was ready, we would make a fortune selling it to the shipping industry, but without my knowledge, Reny dumped his shares to some off-shore, government-owned corporation. The tanker wrecking off Scotland's coast ruined me. All the liability was on my shoulders."

"I remember seeing on the news the devastation of the animal life and the coastline," Martha added, her voice soft. "Men lost their lives, too."

Edwin's pistol arm dropped completely. His face sagged, melting into an expression of haggard grief. Turning his head, Edwin's gaze came to rest on Helen.

"Reny was about to do it again," he said, his words sounding raspy, his complexion reddening, "with the help of Senator Anderson, his corrupt father-in-law, and you and your husband, Mrs. Cousins."

There was a deathlike silence in the van. Helen's mind raced to the conversations she'd heard between Piers and Reny about the financial backing Reny was seeking from Piers. It was for an aviation navigational software. Reny had said it was a sure-fire money-maker because the government would make it mandatory on any plane flying within US airspace. Helen's stomach twisted with revulsion.

"Edwin," she said once she found her voice, "Piers and I would never, never have wanted to be a part of something so filthy. Is that why you tried to make it look like we'd killed Reny?"

As she waited for his answer, she saw Sasha's face peek around the door's opening. Mufidy roused, a low groan coming from where he sat in the driver's seat. Edwin, reaching over, whacked him like he was taking care of an irritating fly buzzing about the old van. Helen and Martha jumped and cringed at the brutal action. Turning back to Helen, his manner almost casual, Edwin continued.

"To be fair, Mrs. Cousins, I didn't want to kill Reny. I wanted him to pay, to be humiliated, and hopefully go to jail. But something snapped. His indifference and cavalier attitude over the horrible evil he'd unleashed on the world, the people he'd killed and the lives he'd ruined meant nothing to him. Tossing those chips at me was the last straw. I bashed him over the head with the first thing I grabbed, the clothes steamer. Later, I hoped the police would believe your husband to be the murderer. Why not? He's another greedy bastard who wants to make money no matter what the cost. It was Matteo who pointed the police in your direction by stating he'd overheard you arguing with Reny. The cards fell where they may—at your feet, Mrs. Cousins, instead of your husband's."

Helen sat mute, but Martha pushed on.

"By now they'll have figured out it wasn't Helen."

Edwin blurted, "Why so?"

With a casual nonchalance, Martha quipped, "She's a lefty. Whoever used the steamer was right-handed."

Edwin blinked a few times as if coming to grips with Martha's revelation about Helen's obvious innocence. He shrugged it off and gave a short, almost congenial chuckle.

"No, Mrs. Littleword, trust me. After this is finished today, they'll believe it was her."

Helen came back to life.

"Why are we in Scotland, Edwin?" she asked. "If not for the Holinshed, why?"

"Mrs. Cousins, things are rarely what they seem in life. Even Sasha Pelletier hasn't been exactly honest about her dealings with you. I'll grant you, we played her, but it was a true piece of genius using Reny's daughter as a pawn in his downfall."

Martha and Helen exchanged wary glances.

"Not exactly honest?" Helen echoed. "How so?"

"She was told to request your expertise in ascertaining the legitimacy of a manuscript, a rare edition of The Holinshed Chronicles, correct?"

Helen nodded. Out of the corner of her eye she caught in the passenger door's rear-view mirror Sasha slipping along the van's side toward the back of the vehicle.

Edwin laughed out loud, apparently enjoying the joke to which only he had the punch line.

"No Holinshed, Mrs. Cousins. Something much more valuable and Ms. Pelletier knew it. She proved her integrity by not selling a stolen Swedish map, so we knew she would stay true to her client confidentiality agreement. Too much was at stake."

"Were you Sasha's client? The one she's come to believe was her father?" Martha asked.

Edwin nodded.

"Yes, Sasha fell into my lap, so to speak. She showed up on a DNA test."

Martha shook her head back and forth.

"How would you have access to Reny Redfern's DNA?"

"Coraliss Redfern."

Martha's eyebrows popped upward.

"You and Coraliss are together?"

Edwin's aspect went mask-like again, but he answered never-the-less.

"Not exactly, more like partners. We both wanted something from Reny. Coraliss wanted children, but Reny wouldn't allow it. Naturally, she wondered why and lighted on the idea he may already have children. A brilliant creature herself, Coraliss collected enough drool from him while asleep to send off to one of those online ancestry companies. Bingo! There was Sasha. At first, it hurt her, and she wanted out of her marriage, but leaving Reny meant she'd walk without a dime."

"How did you and Coraliss hook up, so to speak?" Martha asked.

"She found me. Coraliss is exceedingly bright and inquisitive. It's in her nature. Being a senator's daughter, she had to survive one way or another. About a year ago, she'd overheard her father and Reny discussing a new project. With Anderson's congressional influence, Reny said, they'd make a mint. He said he'd done it before. They would make their money and if complications arose, like what happened in Scotland, they would bail. That's all it took. Coraliss investigated what happened in Scotland and found me. She wanted out of her marriage, I wanted revenge and we both wanted money. Reny wasn't someone you blackmailed. We needed something so valuable, he'd be putty in our hands."

"Is that why you brought Sasha and me into this?" Helen asked.

"It had to look credible. Our sting on Reny needed the proper players, the art market, the academics like you, Mrs. Cousins, and Sir Barstow. Sasha was the rabbit to bring in the fox, after all, she was his daughter. He was curious once Coraliss told him about her, so he hired an investigator to find out more. He knew she worked at Fordham's, tried to bring her under his control by hiring her to help buy the Swedish map, and for this con of ours, Coraliss made sure he knew Sasha was the one brokering the deal."

"For a Holinshed?" Helen asked. "It's rare, but with Reny's money, something he could pick up easily from the right dealer."

Edwin laughed and shook his head.

"No, a much bigger fish was the bait to bring in Reny."

"What are we going to see at Mr. McMurray's, Edwin?" Helen asked. "It must be big indeed."

Edwin's face brightened with a benevolent smile.

"The holy grail of lost medieval manuscripts, Mrs. Cousins... the lost section of The Book of Kells."

Chapter Thirty-Nine

"Look at all the press vehicles!"

The words rushed out of Lucy McCreedie with a whoosh of air as she and Johns drove along the A82 outside of the town of Fort Augustus. "Oh, I'm not sure about this at all—not at all! I won't have to talk to any of these people, will I?"

Hastily turning to Johns, Lucy tried to read his expression but found not one twitch of uncertainty upon his granite-like countenance to hang her growing anxiety upon.

"You won't, no, let me rephrase that." He uncurled a strong-looking index finger from the steering wheel and pointed at the impressive media assembly. "You will *not* be talking to any of *those* people."

Mobile broadcast vans parked alongside the canal, with news reporters milling about and curious onlookers, created a carnival feel to the otherwise tranquil and alpine beauty of Loch Ness.

Feeling slightly sick and wondering if it had been sheer bravado to come and confirm Coraliss Redfern's killer, Lucy scrunched down deeper into her seat, a wave of unease rolling over her.

Around Pitlochry, about half-way into their trip, uncertainty sat in. She hadn't dared to confess her thoughts to the chief inspector sitting beside her.

Putting her head down, she rubbed her temples. What if the man looked nothing like the man she saw on the rocky cliff? What if she saw his face, dead and grey-colored, and she couldn't tell for sure?

"When will I be able to see him?"

Her words were soft, and she wasn't sure of her voice. Out of the corner of her eye, she watched Johns shift in his seat. Could he smell on her a sudden cowardice or worse, the trace of unreliability? A slithering serpent of anxiety lifted its malignant head and coiled itself around her natural confidence.

"Take a deep breath," came Johns' voice, gentle yet firm, "through your nose. Slow down your breathing and remember two things."

She did exactly as he said, clinging to the certainty in his tone and letting the air in her chest fly out with a rush through her mouth.

"We won't be seeing Reny Redfern's body until DCI Moore returns from meeting with Senator Anderson. Most likely that'll be late this evening or tomorrow. Don't worry about your expectations in identifying Redfern as his wife's killer. It may have been too far away, even through binoculars, to be sure of what you saw."

As if his words worked some kind of magic on her, Lucy's heartbeat slowed and she leaned back in the seat, letting her shoulders relax. A confession unbidden from her mind slipped in a whisper from her mouth.

"I was so scared on the hillside after..." she paused testing her sense of stability before she pushed on, "after I saw him push her. He came along the path right above me and I knew, I don't know how I knew, but I did, that if he saw me or heard me, he'd kill me too."

Johns didn't reply. Lucy glanced over at him. His face was unmoving but grim in its aspect. For a moment, she remembered her father. He, too, was a powerfully built man, always solid in his notion of life and how to respond to its challenges. She wished he was still alive. He'd have given her a place to crawl into, a place to feel safe.

Johns, when he finally spoke, used gentle words.

"Lucy, I've worked in this field for many years. When people experience what you did, seeing someone's life brutally taken from them, they need to work through the shock and the fear. Your situation is even more difficult. You were alone and afraid. If you didn't have some anxiety at seeing the killer, whether he's dead or alive, I'd say you were lying."

The panic subsided completely. She wanted to see Reny Redfern. She wanted to know if it was him or not. Tears pooled in her eyes.

"I'm okay," she said with certainty and turning to look at DCI Johns, her eyes glittering with tears.

"I owe it to the woman to do my best. Do you think I'll know if it's him, the one who killed her?"

She waited, worried but hopeful, watching him consider her question.

"Yes," Johns answered, not taking his eyes off the road. "You'll know him. When you see a person kill someone, you never forget either the killer's face or the victim's. It sticks with you forever."

Chapter Forty

At Edwin's revelation, a stunned silence reverberated around the inside of the old grocer's van.

"You believe," Helen started slowly, "that you may have the lost section of The Book of Kells?"

Martha watched Helen's face as she tried to stifle a cynical guffaw. There was a definite intense internal struggle in the woman. When Edwin first made the announcement, Helen did the old jaw drop followed quickly by a huff of disbelief, but Martha knew Helen well. The other side of her friend's nature, the treasure seeker side, was surely pulling at Helen's curiosity.

"That's why you're here, Mrs. Cousins," Edwin shrugged and smiled. "You're the tops in your field and I needed the best. At the moment, you are not expendable."

He casually pointed at Martha with the gun.

"You are expendable."

Using the gun as his preferred pointing tool, Martha wasn't sure if he wanted an answer. Instead, she focused on trying to look small and gave him only a noncommittal shoulder shrug.

With a crisp edge to her voice, Helen said, "Sasha asked how many tickets I wanted. Martha is my colleague and my friend. We work together on everything. It was supposed to be a fun week, a girl's trip."

Helen and Martha looked at each other.

"We gotta quit these kinda 'fun weeks', Helen," Martha said with a tiny chuckle and an encouraging grin.

Helen returned the smile, but her laugh held no mirth.

"Well, if you're finished with the chic-bonding moment, I want you both out of this van and we'll hike the rest of the way to McMurray's house. It's not far up the glen, only about another mile. If it is the lost section of The Book of Kells, I'll be flying out of Inverness tonight."

It was Martha's turn to do the dropped jaw bit.

"You can't leave. It's a murder investigation."

He waved the gun around as if he was shewing invisible flies.

"I'm not concerned, Mrs. Littleword. You've forgotten. They'll believe it was Mrs. Cousins who killed Reny, especially once I return to the boat and tell the police she tried to kill me, too."

"You're insane," Martha blurted.

"No, I'll leave with the manuscript tucked neatly under my arm. Now, get out! I didn't want to hurt anyone, but well, enjoy your walk ladies. It's your last day above ground."

They piled out of the van. Martha was glad she'd dressed down for the meeting with McMurray. If she was to traipse over the mountains, she had the right footwear. Her shoes were vintage combat boots along with black tights, a knit calve-length skirt, and a black velvet, slim-fitting jacket over a silk turtleneck. Helen's attire, though classic, with low pumps and a tailored suit, wasn't ideal for a cross-country hike.

Once she planted her feet firmly on the ground, Helen said, "My shoes won't make it along this goat path. If you want me to look at this supposed lost section, we need to take the van. I won't walk. Besides, Sir Alec Barstow will be there soon."

As Helen dug in her heals, Martha scanned the area for Sasha but came up empty. Wanting to stoop over to see if the young woman was under the van, Martha played the untied shoe ruse. A quick look at the van's underside revealed nothing.

Edwin, like any true southerner from New Orleans, must have recognized when he was up against the will of a southern female. Even if forced to walk, he must have known Helen would try to slow them down. Edwin needed her assessment if he wanted to sell the manuscript, plus the police would come looking for them soon. DCI Moore wouldn't be patient once their group didn't show up this afternoon. She'd send someone to collect them if she hadn't already.

Looking around at the vast, uninhabited landscape, it was clear Edwin wanted them to get moving. Holding out his hand, he demanded, "Hand me your cell phones."

Each woman gave him their phones which he threw into a ravine.

"I don't drive a clutch. Which one of you do?" he asked, his voice rising with frustration.

"I do. Helen can't drive one either," Martha answered, flashing a 'go along with it' glance over at Helen.

It was a bald-faced lie, but it was her only hope of surviving. If Helen could drive, Edwin might see how dispensable she, Martha, really was.

"Yes, I've never learned to drive a car with a clutch," Helen added, perfectly on cue.

Pointing the gun at Martha again, he said, "Go drag Mufidy from the driver's seat and pull him to the back of the van. Tie him up." Turning around, he yelled, "Sasha! I know you're hiding on the other side of those boulders. Get over here!" Turning back to Helen, he said, "You ride in the back."

He went over to the driver's seat and reached into the cab. Taking the keys from the ignition, he mumbled something about answering the call of Mother Nature and went over to Sasha, pulling her out from behind the boulders. Martha watched him take her cell phone, toss it into the ravine and point at the van then disappear, himself, behind the same boulders.

Following instructions, Martha went around the van to find Sasha coming toward her. Their eyes met. Red-cheeked and her jacket pulled as tightly as possible around her slim frame, Sasha looked terrified. An idea flashed into Martha's head.

Scanning the younger woman's attire, it relieved her to see Sasha had dressed comfortably, too. She'd chosen a high-neck sweater that hung to mid-thigh over which she'd put a cropped, tweed jacket complemented by a long scarf wrapped and looped stylishly around her neck. Her thick brown leggings looked warm and her boots had only a one-inch heel.

"Come on, help me move, Mufidy. It'll be okay, Sasha."

Once they were out of earshot of Edwin, Martha, her voice barely audible over the Highland wind, whispered, "I'll leave the van's back door ajar. It'll look shut but be open. When I start the van and take off, I want you to jump out. Run for cover. I'll keep going. If you can, try to flag down a car and get back to the police. Tell them where we are and let Piers know."

With a rattled, horrified expression like Martha had asked her to go skydiving without a parachute, Sasha shook her head rapidly back and forth.

Martha laid her hand on Sasha's arm, applying firm pressure. Locking onto the younger woman's eyes, her tone low and adamant, she said, "You must do this. If you're not his accomplice, he's going to kill you. He may kill you anyway. Do what I say and we might all live."

Tears pooled in the girl's eyes, but she nodded. Swallowing hard, she said, "Okay, I'll do it."

Martha offered her an encouraging smile and patted her arm.

"Help me with Mufidy."

The Caledonian Queen's mechanic was as solid as a Highland boulder. Helen lent a hand and with all three women pushing and hoisting, they laid Mufidy on his side up against the ribbed wall.

"I hope he's okay," Sasha said. "I know he's important to Emily."

"He's breathing," Helen answered in the same hushed way. "Use the bungee cords to secure him so he doesn't roll about the floor. Let's shove those towels under his head."

Martha heard Edwin coming around to the passenger side door. Crouched together in a huddle over Mufidy, she whispered in Helen's ear the plan for Sasha to leave the van through the back as quietly as possible and go for help.

"I'll pull the door shut," Helen whispered back.

With Mufidy secure and everyone taking their places, Martha patted around on him. With the deftness of a first-rate London pickpocket, Martha found what she wanted, secreted it in her jacket's pocket, and hurriedly crawled into the driver's seat.

Shooting Edwin a sour look for good measure, she held out her hand to receive the keys. After a few grumblings and two loud backfires, the old greengrocer's van jumped forward and plunged down the road renewing its moaning, clanging, and whining about life's hardships, a perfect cover for Sasha's escape.

Tight-lipped and with a death-grip on the steering wheel, Martha pushed down on the gas pedal bringing the van up to five miles an hour. With a furtive look through the rearview mirror, she caught Sasha slipping out the back. Helen pulled the door shut, giving a thumbs-up to Martha.

It was time to put some distance between them and Sasha. Pushing down on the gas pedal, Martha brought the van up to a nearly impossible speed causing Edwin to grip the dashboard and stare at the road ahead. Sasha's exit was undetected and a success.

"Which way?" Martha asked casually.

A fork in the road revealed itself as they plunged down the hillside.

"To the right and you can see the top of the house over the ridge."

A few more stolen glances at her driver's side mirror told Martha Sasha was nowhere to be seen. Taking a deep breath, she held it for a second and prayed internally.

"Dear God, if you can hear me... okay, that was stupid, of course, you can hear me. Please, please, please let Sasha be on the up and up. Let her find help. I promise to quit all potato chips and forgive Merriam for being a jerk if you'll get Helen and me out of this."

Martha always liked to give a sign-off.

"Thank you, Big Guy. Love ya."

On a wing and a prayer, the greengrocer van made a right at the fork in the road and bounced more than drove toward McMurray's house. Martha had been right, she reflected. The drive had been, in every sense, one heck of a bumpy ride.

Chapter Forty-One

Coraliss Redfern's face was surprisingly serene, showing no sign of her last terrifying seconds on Earth. Around her gurney stood DCI Moore, Senator Anderson, and Special Agent Quinn solemnly gazing on the pretty blonde, her eyes shut in eternal sleep. The only thing marring Coraliss' otherwise unblemished face was a blue and black contusion smeared across her forehead and up into her scalp. A spotless, white sheet concealed the rest of her body, hiding any hint of the brutal wounds beneath.

Quinn and Moore excused themselves and went to the outer corridor, leaving the senator alone with his dead and only daughter. Once out of ear reach, they took up positions on opposite walls. Quinn broke the silence first, keeping his voice low.

"Would you be willing, DCI Moore, to share some information regarding your investigation of Reny Redfern's death?"

Verity watched him glance surreptitiously through the doors where Senator Anderson stood with his back to them. An old familiar tingle at the tip of her nose made her reach up and quickly, unconsciously give it a rub with the edge of her index finger. It was always a precursor or an instinctual hint a case had more to its depth, more secrets to its story.

"If sharing information," she gestured with a flick of her hand meaning he would need to share, too, "will benefit both of my murder investigations, I'd be happy to assist the FBI. What would you like to know?"

Again, the hurried glance to be sure Anderson hadn't moved.

"We wondered if any papers or laptop belonging to Reny Redfern might be available for our inspection."

Quinn closed the gap between Verity's wall and his.

"We've been looking into Reny Redfern's business interests. With his death and his wife's, we would finally have access to their emails and correspondence. It's an internal government matter, but with possible global reach."

Rolling her lips up into a thoughtful pucker at the corner of her mouth, Verity considered Quinn's vague statement. His body language and furtive glances at Anderson, a US senator setting on multiple regulatory committees, told her so much more.

If the senator was being 'looked into' by the FBI, they would get their information on him one way or the other, with or without her help. She pushed for clarity.

"In the van, Senator Anderson asked about Mr. Redfern's belongings. He wanted to know if we found any items such as a laptop or briefcase among his things."

Moore watched Quinn's reaction. He was overly still.

"I will tell you what I told Senator Anderson. Mr. Redfern came on The Caledonian Queen with a friend, Mr. Piers Cousins who lives in a village in Yorkshire. They drove together and came on the cruise as a spur-of-the-moment decision. Among Mr. Redfern's personal items, we found no briefcase or laptop."

"Where did the passengers leave their vehicles?" Quinn quickly asked.

"Fort William. There is a dock area with secure parking. Any items Reny Redfern may have left in Mr. Cousins' car will be evidence in my murder investigation."

Quinn nodded in agreement.

"Should be interesting…" he said, but the sound of the doors opening halted any further conversation between the two.

"I want to head back to Washington after seeing Reny. My secretary will make the arrangements for Coraliss' body."

"Senator, I would like to get a formal statement from you before you leave. It would help our investigation if you would please share any information regarding the last days of your daughter's life."

Anderson shoved his hands into the front pockets of his trousers and scowled. His face flushed red, and he drew air into his lungs, locking onto Moore with his eyes.

"I spoke with my daughter the night before she must have died. She was unhappy with me because I disagreed with her desire to leave her husband."

"Did she say why she wanted to leave Mr. Redfern?"

"No," Anderson said firmly. "She claimed Reny was having an affair and that he was…well, that he was often…unkind. I didn't take her seriously. I thought she was trying to stack the deck in her favor."

"Do you believe your daughter may have taken her own life?" Moore asked.

She gave him a moment to consider this question. It was the second time she'd asked him. A part of Verity wanted to block Johns' involvement in her case. If Coraliss Redfern jumped from the cliff, Johns would be relegated to the same place as the press—the sidelines.

Without hesitation, Anderson answered, "Absolutely not. I don't believe Coraliss would have done that to herself." He paused and ran one hand through his hair. "She told me she wanted to be free of Reny."

Verity couldn't ignore the obvious. Anderson's word 'unkind' sounded like a man downplaying a truth. An irritating twinge of uncertainty needled Moore's brain, flashing a warning sign to her ego. As much as she hated it, she would have to accept the involvement of Lucy McCreedie and her white knight, Merriam Johns. Verity hadn't made DCI by not following through on every angle, statement, or motive innate to a case.

"Sir, what did you mean about your daughter saying her husband could be unkind?"

Quinn's eyebrows raised at the question.

"I ask this question for a reason. Your daughter wasn't alone on her hike. I have a witness that saw her with a man on the outcropping seconds before she fell to her death. The same witness helped the emergency crew find her."

"Who is this witness?" Anderson demanded. "What did they see exactly?"

"It is a young woman, a bird watcher, out for a day from Edinburgh. She saw them through her binoculars. It's nothing provable, but she believes she saw a man resembling Mr. Redfern push your daughter from the cliff."

Anderson looked like she'd punched him in the stomach. He swayed, reaching out for the wall to support himself. Hanging his head like a man who'd lost the will to stand upright, he groaned, "Reny? Is this woman sure?"

"We'll know in about an hour. She's coming to Fort Augustus to make the identification at the clinic where his body is being held until authorities can transfer it to Inverness. That's why I've asked you about your daughter's relationship with her husband. Did you ever question yourself about his behavior or consider his actions to be dangerous or worrisome? Was he a man who might hurt without remorse?"

Senator Anderson raised his head. Moore watched as in excellent politician form; he pulled his mental and physical being together before committing to an answer.

"Reny was a businessman," he finally conceded. "He hunted, and he competed to win in everything he did, but a dangerous man or one who hurts without remorse?"

The senator rolled the statement up at the end, turning her

question into his question. As if he'd only considered Reny's real nature for the first time today. At last, he shook his head and dropped his eyes from hers.

"I can honestly say, I have no knowledge of Reny ever doing anything dishonest, hurtful, or dangerous to another person."

It was the personal involvement disclaimer politicians the world over always used, but Verity caught the first truth in his eyes before he looked at the floor.

Anderson was a liar, but how much of one?

"We need you to come to Fort Augustus, senator, to identify his body. The press will be there, and we would appreciate you not mentioning anything regarding what you've learned so far, but your identification of your son-in-law is necessary. We've had other people state they believe it to be Reny Redfern, but only one person onboard The Caledonian Queen says they knew him, a Mr. Piers Cousins. However, this gentleman hadn't truly seen him since university. Your identification would be pivotal to our investigation."

Taking a step away from the wall, Verity watched as he straightened himself up to his full height.

"Let's go," he said, "I want to get it over with and I want to know if this birdwatcher can truly point the finger at Reny for killing my daughter. If she does, Reny's lucky to be dead."

The good senator took the lead and headed down the hallway with Quinn taking up the rear. Both men disappeared around a corner. Hearing the door bang shut, Moore waited, giving a last look through the windows at the body on the gurney and pondering the young life cut short.

If Reny Redfern killed his wife, she thought, he did it for gain, out of jealously or because she'd threatened to ruin him.

"I think your father knows more than he's letting on?" Verity murmured to the lifeless Coraliss.

"In fact, I think he's tied up with your husband in something illegal or immoral. Quinn does, too. Let's see if we can get it out of him, shall we? I owe you that."

Turning away, Verity walked down the hall, her mind playing back her and Quinn's earlier conversation. A smile slowly crept across her face.

"I would have never thought of it. Thanks, Quinn. I can hardly wait to see what's in Piers Cousins' car boot."

Chapter Forty-Two

Arthur McMurray and Sir Alec Barstow watched the rattletrap of a greengrocer van rumble down the mountain road. It bounced about on either two wheels or three, but rarely as they watched did all four wheels at the same time appear to be in contact with the ground. The driver's method was the same as that of a mountain biker's, get to the bottom as fast as possible by the most direct route.

The two men had been sitting and enjoying an excellent Scottish liqueur neatly over ice, discussing the manuscript which Sir Alec had long since finished inspecting when the sound of backfiring and a loud engine approaching forced them to turn in unison and direct their attention outside. Swiveling their comfortable chairs to face the nice-sized picture window, both men watched with bemused amazement the van's progress.

"Surely that is not Helen Ryes Cousins?" Sir Alec asked. "I'd have expected a Range Rover."

"It is odd," Arthur conceded, "but to be honest, I've seen stranger things arrive and deposit visitors at my gate. Donkeys, horses, a wide range of utility vehicles, and even one helicopter have been used to traverse these mountains, but never what must be a milk or grocery van."

Exchanging mildly amused expressions, the two men put down their drinks and hurried outside.

They'd barely made the front step, when the van, at the bottom of the incline leading up to Arthur's cottage, sputtered and coughed. It chugged a few more yards uphill, but as the gradient must have been too much for it, the tired van expelled one mighty exploding backfire and died.

The cacophony of metallic sounds, like the end of a symphony, came to their rollicking finale. Perfect silence ensued. Edwin turned around in his seat. Helen watched as he cast his gaze around the van's interior.

"Where is Sasha?" he asked, his face growing red.

"She jumped from the back about ten minutes ago," Helen said, her anger rising to meet his.

"You let her go?" he growled, getting up from his seat.

Martha held up her hand to stop him.

"Helen couldn't have stopped her, Edwin," she said, her voice low. "She's probably out wandering these mountains. God help her. She's likely to topple off a precipice before she finds another human."

Helen knew Martha was planting a seed of doubt about Sasha's ability to make it over the mountains and find help. It would slow Edwin's anger. Best if she, Helen, threw her weight behind Martha's plan.

"Sasha is long gone, Edwin. I don't know why she jumped, but this is *not* the time to hash it out. We need to get out of this," Helen looked around the van's inside, "vile piece of metal trash that ever rode on four worthless wheels and appraise your supposed manuscript. I'm sick of your bullying. If you want this done, let's go!"

Helen knew he had no choice. Turning on Martha, he almost hissed.

"Did the van die? Will it restart?"

"I let it die," she answered calmly. "It has gas and will restart. Should make it back fine."

"Okay," he said, "let not try anything stupid, ladies. Get out and don't be heroes. Remember, I have a gun with me."

Helen glanced down at Mufidy's bound body. Leaning over him, she listened for his breathing. Thankfully, it sounded normal. If Sasha was successful, the paramedics would be here soon.

Helen pushed the back door open and taking hold of the frame, stepped free of the van. Hidden from view, she performed a quick smoothing of her clothes and hair. She walked around from behind the van to see Sir Alec waiting at the top of the cottage's steps.

He waved heartily. A knot tightened in her stomach. She and Martha must do everything in their power to keep him safe.

"Sir Alec!" she called up to him, putting on a bright smile. "How wonderful it is to see you!"

With a quick look at Martha's reflection through the driver's side mirror, who was applying lipstick in the van's rearview mirror, Helen mentally congratulated Martha on her power to achieve the extraordinary at the most challenging of moments.

"Your choice of vehicle, my dear Helen, tells me you have a fascinating story to relate," Sir Alec called, his face beaming with delight. "However, you look as beautiful as ever!"

Martha stepped free from the van as Helen came up to her driver's door. The Cambridge professor clapped his hands together with pleasure and navigated the stone steps leading down to them. The last time he'd worked with Martha, they hit it off, both enjoying a fun, sparkling new friendship.

"Mrs. Littleword," he said, "so you are the daredevil driver of that jalopy. We watched your precipitous descent and marveled at your spirited driving skill. Quite the entertainment! Edge of my seat stuff!"

He paused for a moment, scanning the area, most likely trying to assess Sasha's whereabouts. He lifted his eyebrows and chin; the smile dimming.

"It's a pleasant surprise, Mrs. Littleword. I didn't expect you. Where is Sasha? Is she not coming today?"

Martha, her tone easy and light, replied first.

"She wasn't feeling her best, Sir Alec. We left her behind on the boat. It might be a touch of seasickness."

He appeared to accept this excuse with his natural grace, old-world manners, and good humor.

"Oh, too bad, too bad! Sasha will have wished she'd braved the drive and the indisposition," he said, shaking his head and giving her a knowing wink. "I cannot wait for you to lay your eyes upon the pages waiting for you. Come! Come!"

He turned and beckoned them to follow him up the path, talking the entire way about Gaelic monasticism.

There was nothing to do, Helen determined mentally, but to play her part. Martha had beautifully managed the question of Sasha's absence, but what if Sasha wasn't trustworthy? It was obvious Edwin had a plan for the manuscript, but Sasha needed it, too. How did she fit into this story?

Helen shook her head slightly to clear her thoughts and hoped Mr. McMurray who stood up at the cottage's front door hadn't noticed the odd action. What would happen once they'd finished their appraisal?

"This must be Mr. McMurray," Martha said, holding her hand out for the man to take. "It is nice to meet you."

"The pleasure is mine," he answered, shaking Martha's hand and turning to Helen. "Mrs. Cousins, thank you both for coming all this way. I'm sorry Ms. Pelletier isn't here."

"Let me introduce, Edwin Montfort," Helen said, trying to explain Edwin's presence. "He's a guest from The Caledonian Queen, the cruise boat we've been traveling on. We picked him up along the way. The ill weather cut his hiking trip short."

Never before had Helen introduced a sociopathic killer to anyone, but she and Martha both offered gracious smiles as Mr. McMurray nodded at Edwin, saying, "Please come inside and let me offer you some refreshment. You must need something warm after traveling so far in that old van. The manuscript is on the table in the lounge."

They followed him and Sir Alec. Inside, a warm lounge area awaited where McMurray pointed to a table. Many loose leaves of an old manuscript lay upon it.

"Here it is, Mrs. Cousins," he said, his face beaming with pride.

Helen smiled weakly and approached the table. At least twenty vellum pages roughly the same size as a piece of normal copy paper, but larger by an inch or two both vertically and horizontally, lay on the table. Some bound and some not, all showed signs of deterioration. Decorated in an exceptionally ornate, early medieval style, they were written in a Latin text known as Insular script. Colorful geometric designs in various Celtic knotwork patterns framed the pages. It was stunning, and in many places, Helen noted evidence of water damage.

"I need to wash my hands before I touch them. May I use your bathroom, Mr. McMurray?" she asked.

Ignoring Edwin's, "Is that necessary?" Helen followed her host down a short hallway. She heard Martha and Sir Alec discussing the importance of clean hands when touching manuscripts.

"It's in here." He opened the door to the restroom. "Mrs. Cousins, may I ask your initial opinion of the documents?"

She blinked at him once or twice, compressing her mouth as she thought what her best answer would be.

"To be accurate, we need to perform diagnostic tests on manuscripts of this caliber. I thought I'd be looking at something entirely different today. This has come as a surprise, Mr. McMurray. I didn't come prepared to assess something so rare. If these are early Celtic Christian illuminated manuscripts, Sir Alec will need to have them evaluated by other scholars. The first thing should be to notify Scotland's National Trust or the cultural governing body who manages rare finds."

A shadow descended upon McMurray's face.

"But you and Sir Alec should be able to give an opinion, yes?"

She would have explained further how it was an impossible task to validate a manuscript like this one without a team of scholars, forensic scientists, and a laboratory of specialized equipment, but it was pointless at the moment. Sir Alec knew it also.

Helen offered McMurray a faint smile.

"Give me a minute. I'll be right out."

As he nodded and turned to walk back to the lounge, Helen's heart did a jump in her chest. There along the baseboard ran a white phone cable. Mr. McMurray had a landline.

Quickly she washed her hands and dried them thoroughly. Slipping out the door as quietly as possible, Helen followed the cable down the hall until she came to the kitchen. There, on the wall, in all its 1990s glory, hung a cordless phone with an antenna. Grabbing it, she found the ringer button on the base, switched it off and hurried back to the bathroom.

Shutting the door, she turned on the water and flushed the toilet to make it look good. Her fingers easily dialed Piers' number and waited through each successive ring, expecting to be found out at any moment.

"Hello?" came Piers' voice.

"Piers, listen. Edwin Montfort is insane. He killed Reny and he's got Sir Alec, Martha and me in this cottage somewhere up in the mountains."

"Helen?" Piers asked. "Is that you?"

Taken aback for a moment, she held the phone out to see if it was working.

"Of course, it's me," she nearly cried. "Get the police and tell them we are somewhere west of Tomchrasky in a cottage possibly owned by a man named Arthur McMurray."

A knock on the bathroom door made her almost drop the phone.

"Helen?"

It was Sir Alec.

"Yes!" she answered. "I'm sorry. I'll be right out. I wasn't feeling well."

Into the phone, she whispered, "Piers, please hurry. I've got to go."

Seeing a basket of hand towels, she pushed the button to turn off the phone and stuffed it beneath the pile of towels.

Washing her hands one more time, she went back to the lounge. All eyes turned to her. Going over to where her purse sat on the table, Helen took out her magnifying glasses, a tape measurer, and a hand-held light from her case. On the table lay the fragile-looking manuscript and loose pages. Putting on her glasses, she approached the table.

The most arresting page, one depicting the crucifixion of Christ, she reached for. Lifting it, Helen studied the blue pigments decorating the design work. If these manuscript pages were originals from the Book of Kells, they should have key, defining elements about them. Without the right tests, there was no way to be sure of the pigments. She focused on the blue used within the designs. It was deep and intense.

Picking up her measuring tape, she first measured the length and the width of the leaves. Something wasn't adding up. Helen stepped back from the table and turned to Sir Alec. He was wearing a pursed mouth and twinkling eyes. He'd seen it, too.

"I believe there is something amiss here," Helen said. "The vellum leaves are larger than the ones currently included in The Book of Kells at Trinity College. This would give credence to your case that these are the lost leaves, but the blue pigment is extremely vivid."

"We'll need a pigment analysis," Sir Alec said. "Look at this page, Helen. Tell me what you think."

He gently turned the book over to show Helen the last few leaves. Though her Latin wasn't up to the level of Sir Alec's, she deciphered enough to know it was a summary by the scribe who finished the manuscript. It was as follows:

THE PSALTER IS FINISHED. IN CHRIST OUR LORD, READ IN PEACE. Like a timely harbour to sailors is the last line to scribes. Æthelberht, son of Berhtfrith, wrote this gloss. Whoever may read it, may he pray for the scribe. And he himself similarly desires eternal health for all people, tribes and tongue and for the entire human race. In Christ, Amen, Amen, Amen.

"It's a colophon," Helen breathed.

She looked up at Sir Alec. Their eyes met, and a thrill of sheer wonder crackled between them. The Cambridge scholar nodded.

"Telling, don't you think?" he asked. "That particular scribe is found working on other manuscripts associated with Northumbria during the eighth century. He uses a similar colophon in one other manuscript I know of."

Edwin walked around to stand between the two of them. He took the vellum leaf from Helen's hand and laid it on the table.

"Are you saying, you both won't confirm the validity of this manuscript?"

There was something quiet and chilling about his manner.

"We're *saying* something is unusual about what we see in front of us," Sir Alec said, his tone that of a suspicious academic.

"Please explain," Edwin said, flashing a look at Arthur.

Sir Alec drew himself up straighter, stuffed his hands in his jacket's pockets, and drew an easy breath as if he was about to lecture a group of his students.

"My first inclination steers me to believe these are excellent copies of originals, extraordinary copies. Whoever did them is a master. I suspect this based on the colophon and the size of the vellum. The original Book of Kells at Trinity has been cut down once. Your leaves are larger. As, you asked for my opinion on a Holinshed, but gave me these loose leaves to consider instead, it would seem someone wanted to do a test drive, so to speak, of their handy work by having Helen and I come all this way. But more to your point, if your copyist has used lapis lazuli instead of indigo from the Indigofera species, they made a mistake."

McMurray's response was swift.

"I disagree! All scholarly articles mention the use of lapis lazuli."

"No." Sir Alec was firm. "Recent tests using micro-Raman spectroscopy confirm the predominant use of indigo."

Edwin slammed his fist down on the table.

"I told you to do your research on the pigments used!" he yelled at McMurray.

"I did! Fifteen years ago, when I started these," McMurray said with a sweeping gesture of the leaves lying on the table. "Back then, scholars believed monks used lapis lazuli."

Helen, like a barometer sensing the approach of a storm, laid her hand on Sir Alec's forearm and with a gentle pressure pulled him back from between the two arguing men. They went to stand beside Martha.

Edwin grabbed the manuscript into his arms and walked over to the fireplace where a warm peat fire was burning in its grate.

"These are all useless."

"Stop!" Sir Alec demanded, halting Edwin's destruction.

There was a groan from McMurray.

"I worked on those for years! For years!"

Edwin dropped the pages and pulled the gun from his pocket, pointing it at the assembly.

"Go collect the originals, Arthur. There is no time. The buyer expected something, and he's not someone to disappoint. We'll sell the originals instead. Take these three to the underground cell."

McMurray looked stricken. His face melted into one of horror and disbelief.

"To the cell?" he whispered, glancing worriedly in Helen, Martha, and Sir Alec's direction.

Edwin did a sweeping gesture with the gun taking in the copied manuscript on the table and the three people standing near the window.

"They're all useless to us now. Take your worthless copies, those three experts, and roll a rock over them. Meet me at the van. By the way, you're driving."

Chapter Forty-Three

The evening skies above her were a mixture of purples, grays and pale blues. Over the last hour, the rain had moved out toward the East, leaving behind crystal-clear vistas of the wild landscape stretching out before her. The sun would set behind the mountains soon. As Sasha walked along the dirt road, she hugged her banged-up arm. It felt broken but holding it close was keeping her warm.

All of nature, in its busy summer activity, was quieting down for the evening. Only the wind kept up a relentless buffeting of the pink heather carpeting the land, the spiny gorse bushes populating the sides of the road, and the conical-shaped, green spruces tucked back into craggy, boulder-born habitats.

It was beautiful but lonely finding her way back. Not one car had come along the road. She wasn't despairing yet, though. It was late summer, and tourists and freight traffic would be thick once she made it to the highway.

At the top of a hill, her gaze clapped upon the valley stretching out beneath her. A ribbon of gray asphalt, the main road to Fort Augustus, wound its way through the glen.

"Thank you!" she exclaimed.

Hurrying, Sasha achieved the intersection and turned eastward toward the villages she knew to be a few miles down the road. A compact car followed by a lorry both whizzed past her before she had time to flag them down.

"I need one person to stop. One person with a mobile phone. Please, please dear God, just one."

The walking was easy along the road. With a fiery glow illuminating the western horizon, Sasha stopped. The beauty surrounding her was impossible to ignore. As if all of nature was playing in perfect harmony, she bowed her head and shook it.

"If I don't get help soon, it will be too late. TOO LATE!" she yelled up at the heavens. "TOO LATE! I need some help, PLEASE!"

The cry reverberated back and forth against the two rock ravines in which she stood. Birds, already roosted for the night, flew up from their resting places, crying at being disturbed. As they settled back into their nests, she heard an engine's whine coming up the hill.

Hurrying to the middle of the road, Sasha waited. Two headlamps rose over a low hill, scanning the rock wall like a searchlight in an old forties film. The car appeared, its speed at least fifty miles an hour. Sasha didn't hesitate. Jumping up and down, waving her arms, she had no intention of letting this one go past her.

The car swerved, brakes groaned, and tires grabbed, spewing gravel out and away from the car. As it came to a stop on the road's shoulder, Sasha hurried over and peered down into the window. The glass retracted into the door's frame, revealing a kind, familiar face.

"Hey!" Sergeant McBride called. "You're Sasha Pelletier. Thank God I found you. I've been driving up and down these roads trying to find an Arthur McMurray's cottage."

With his words, it was as if her entire being wanted to crumble where she stood. Exhaustion, fear, and the cold were taking their toll. She offered a feeble smile.

"Helen Cousins, Mrs. Littleword, and another colleague of

mine are in great danger. We've got to get help. They're being held at gunpoint by Edwin Montfort."

McBride blinked once at her words and threw open the passenger side door.

"Get in, miss," McBride called to her over the wind. "Let's go get help."

Chapter Forty-Four

Martha watched closely the expression on Arthur McMurray's face. Clearly, he didn't want any part of Edwin's roll-a-rock-over-the-nice-people scheme. Arthur picked up two of the manuscript's pages and pressed them to his chest like loved children.

"I don't want to hurt anyone," he said, his eyebrows knitting with worry as he flashed the group an anxious look.

"You'll do exactly what I say, Arthur," Edwin said, his tone icy. "If you don't, I'll explain to our client why he's not getting his product. Granted, we would have sold him copies, but you screwed that up with the wrong pigment, so now we have no choice. He's already floated us a lot of money to procure the originals and he shall *have* them." Pointing at Helen, Martha, and Sir Alec, he added, "If I allow these people to live, our man in Dubai will have our guts for garters. It might become an international incident. Understand, Arthur? We're in too deep."

"*You're* in too deep, Edwin" McMurray slammed back.

For a second he released the two vellum leaves from his deep embrace and gazed down upon them. He sighed.

"I won't do anything more. You promised the originals would never go out of Scotland. I should have never believed you."

Arthur looked like a man sinking in on himself. With a limp, casual hand, Edwin pointed the gun at Sir Alec.

"It's simple, do as I say, or I'll kill him first."

Any earlier resolve Arthur may have had, evaporated. With another hurried, guilty glance in their direction, he turned away.

"I'll go get a flashlight," he said. "It's getting dark and the walk is difficult."

As he left the room, Helen asked, "Do you really have the original lost section of The Book of Kells?"

"I do," Edwin answered and dipped the pistol back in his pocket. "McMurry found them years ago out in some underground, half-fallen in monk's cell. He's an odd bird. Fascinated with archaeology, Viking burials, early Christian history, but his talent, as you've seen, is art forgery. He's been living out here for over fifteen years working on his copies. He intended to make the copy and give the original to the nation, but I'd met up with him seven years ago in a chat room about illuminated manuscripts. The rest is history."

Edwin chuckled to himself.

"You're not really intending to kill us, Edwin," Martha interjected into the lecture.

He took a deep breath and let it out.

"The plan was to use the originals to entice Reny into admitting his involvement in the tanker wreck off Scotland's coast but never really let him have them. The copies would go to my Dubai client who needed your validation. But since we know Arthur used the wrong blue, there's no chance I'd sell them now. The man in Dubai is quite thorough. The originals are too valuable to leave with Arthur or give to the people of Scotland. Coraliss and I will sell them off piece by piece. But now, none of these options will work, and unfortunately, the three of you are a liability. The short answer is, yes, Mrs. Littleword. I've got to get rid of the evidence."

Arthur appeared in the doorway.

"I'm ready. Let's go."

Turning away, Edwin went to the picture window.

"Do what I told you, McMurray."

In Martha's mind, she knew poor Arthur didn't have much chance of surviving the night either. Discretely, she felt inside her jacket's pocket for the item she'd stashed there earlier.

Wherever this underground cell was, it must be a hike to get there. If Arthur led the way, they might plunk him on the head with something or push him down and make a run for it. With a reassuring smile at Sir Alec and Helen, Martha turned and took the lead, falling in behind Arthur.

As they stepped out into the night, a luminous moon flooded the landscape creating silhouettes of the mountains and the trees in the distance. The wind was wild and having great fun whipping and rolling in off the sea in the West. Tall spruce, their branches swaying, looked like giant, shadowy banshees dancing and whispering of deaths to come.

"You go first," Arthur said. "Follow the path up to the left. It's only a few minutes. With the moon, you should be able to see a little."

His foresight ruined Martha's hopes of him proceeding them to the cell. They'd have to wait until they reached their destination to overpower him.

The climb was short and once the group arrived at the hilltop Martha saw the ruins of a stone shelter. Around it, much digging and earth moving had taken place over many years. Bushy grasses and well-established shrubs covered the mounds of dirt.

"Is this where you found the lost section of the manuscript?" she asked Arthur.

"Yes!" he answered with renewed enthusiasm. "Over the centuries, the cell you're about to see was a place for solitary prayer and, during times of attack, used for hiding valuables. Many of these cells have been found all over the British Isles. I believe a group of Ionian monks came here and built this subterranean cell, but they weren't the ones who left my section of The Book here. They would have sent someone to retrieve it if they fled in a hurry. It was far too holy and valuable to them. It's my opinion, someone found this section and tried to hide it here. I found a small pile of coins dating from the Protestant Revolution near the chest in which the manuscript was contained. It had Lord John Stewart's seal upon the lock."

Getting down the slope was tricky, but once at the bottom, Martha saw an opening in the hillside. Arthur motioned them inside. Bending low, she smelled the dank air wafting out from the low aperture. Arthur focused the flashlight's beam along the tight corridor for them to enter. The shuffling of their feet along the ground and the sound of water dripping through the stones above them, made Martha suddenly aware of the possibility of rodents, snakes, and even bats calling this natural retreat their home.

"Have you ever seen snakes down here, Arthur?" she asked.

"One or two," he answered. "But bats and mice mainly."

"Great," Helen grumbled.

"Arthur," Sir Alec said, his tone congenial and diplomatic, "you have only committed the crime of not relinquishing found cultural items of value back to the nation. If you compound that crime with the one of willful murder, not only will you spend the rest of your days locked inside a prison, but you'll have a heavy burden of guilt upon your spirit. Let us go, Arthur, and I'm sure the authorities will take your act of protecting us into consideration when they hand down their sentence."

Martha had come into a low ceiling vault-like room followed by Helen, Sir Alec, and finally Arthur.

"I promise to not hurt you," Arthur answered.

"Please don't leave us without light," Helen asked.

"Not to worry, dear Helen, I've got my matches for my pipe," Sir Alec said.

With a gallant flair, he took out from his waistcoat a small box of matches and struck one.

"Have you a candle or something, Arthur, before you leave us to our fate?"

Their captor walked over to the side of the sloping stone wall and rustled around in a pile of discarded wood. Helen followed.

"I don't want to leave you here. As soon as I'm able, I'll have someone come for you. I wish, Mrs. Cousins, you'd never mentioned the pigment. It would have been so much better for you."

"I know," Helen answered. "Arthur, I'd like to make this easy for *you*. I know you don't want to hurt us. For that reason alone, you should..."

Martha watched in disbelief as Helen lifted a good-sized stick of wood and brought it down on the back of Arthur's head, sending him into a crumple on the floor.

"...take a nap to think about it," Helen finished.

Sir Alec's eyebrows shot up, his lower jaw dropped, and he gawked at the sprawling, unconscious Arthur.

"You dropped him, Helen!" Martha exclaimed, clapping her hands together and smiling from ear to ear.

Helen looked down and curled up the corner of her mouth in an appreciative smile like she was observing a sleeping baby.

"I did! I dropped him!"

"Guess this will prove you didn't kill Reny," Martha added. "I mean they'll see you do your best work with your left hand."

Both women nodded and burst out with brief chuckles.

"True, true," Helen agreed. "He's down for now and probably safer. Edwin would have killed him probably. We've got to get Edwin before he gets us or tells the police he has proof I was the one who killed Reny."

Sir Alec swung his head back and forth between the two women.

"Didn't kill Reny? Who's Reny and why are you being accused of killing him?" he choked out.

Martha and Helen turned their combined attention onto Sir Alec, but it was Martha who answered.

"Reny *was* a cruel profiteer, extortionist, and psychopath. Edwin killed him, but the police believe it was Helen."

Martha pointed down at Arthur.

"We are witnesses, Sir Alec. Helen prefers to use a left-handed swing when clubbing people over the head."

"Let's get out of here," Helen said, picking up the flashlight. "We've got to stop Edwin before he tries to sell those originals. Any ideas?"

"He's not going anywhere in the van," Martha said.

"Why not?" Helen asked.

Reaching into her pocket, Martha retrieved the keys and dangled them from her fingers.

"He'll have to hoof it out of here if he wants to go."

It was Helen's turn to clap her hands together, her face lighting up with a bright grin, but it was Sir Alec who was the most delighted.

"I could kiss you this instant, you clever thief!" he cried.

"Well, if you like that Alec, you'll love this," Martha said sounding like a game show emcee.

Her two compatriots' eyes widened with expectation.

"What else did you pilfer from Edwin?" Helen practically whispered.

"Not Edwin, Helen," she said reaching into her jacket's pocket, "but Mufidy. I frisked him when Edwin made us tie him up earlier, hoping he'd have one of these on him."

Sir Alec focused the flashlight down onto her hand as Martha uncurled her fingers displaying a perfectly useful and the last of its kind among them, cell phone.

Chapter Forty-Five

J ohns and Lucy sat sipping tea from paper cups in the waiting room of the medical clinic where Reny's body was being temporarily held until the authorities transferred it to Inverness. The receptionist, after hearing they hadn't eaten dinner, made them hot tea, and offered a tin of cookies for sustenance. Food was more of a necessity than a pleasure at the moment and Johns told a reluctant Lucy to eat. It would bolster her energy, he explained, and soothe her anxious stomach.

The phone call to meet DCI Moore came in as they pulled into Fort Augustus. Moore needed Lucy's identification immediately, not tomorrow to move the case forward. On the phone, she told Johns she would be bringing Senator Anderson to the clinic. As the only family member of the deceased, Anderson needed to make the official ID of the body.

An electric mechanism whirring softly into life and the clinic's main entry door sliding back announced Moore's arrival. Johns and Lucy stood up as DCI Moore and two men entered the building. There was no mistaking Senator Anderson. The other man with him looked like a bodyguard or a special agent of some sort.

Separating herself from the men, Moore came forward and offered her hand first to Johns.

"Good to see you, Merriam. Thank you for bringing Miss McCreedie and waiting for me to get here. I'll introduce you to Senator Anderson and Special Agent Quinn of the FBI once Ms. McCreedie has made the ID of Reny Redfern."

Johns nodded affably and after shaking Moore's hand, he said, "It's good to see you, Verity. Ms. McCreedie is ready when you are."

Moore nodded and turning around to address the other two men, she said, "I'll be back in a moment. Please take a seat."

Johns didn't ask to go with Lucy. Shooting a glance at the two men who'd sat at the other end of the waiting room, he instead resumed his seat. The waiting room became as quiet as a true morgue.

Glancing up at the clock hanging on the wall, he realized how late it was getting. Driving back to Edinburgh tonight was out of the question, and there were few hotels in the area. He'd need two rooms, and it was peak tourist season. Chances were slim if he didn't phone soon.

As he pulled his mobile from his coat pocket, he saw he'd missed a call from Piers less than a few minutes ago. The ringer was off. Tapping the messaging icon, he put the phone to his ear to listen.

"I've had a phone call from Helen," Piers said, his tone worried. "She wants me to contact the police. Something's gone wrong with the trip the girls took to visit a man named Arthur McMurray somewhere near Tomchrasky. She says Edwin Montfort has gone off the rails and has admitted to killing Reny Redfern. He wasn't with them when I put them in the van earlier. She's scared. Call me!"

"Martha," Johns murmured, feeling his heartbeat increase. "Those two are magnets for murder and mayhem."

He was dialing Piers when Verity and Lucy reappeared. Looking up at their faces, it was easy to see Reny was indeed Coraliss Redfern's killer. Verity looked sober, and Lucy looked drunk on relief.

"It was him," Lucy said, coming straight to Johns like a child relieved at learning the doctor's visit meant no vaccinations. "You were right about remembering his face. There was no doubt. I knew him immediately."

Johns offered her a reassuring smile.

"Lucy, thank you for making the ID. I'm sure it will help her family to know who her killer was."

Out of the corner of his eye, he saw Senator Anderson stand up and come toward them. They faced him with solemn faces.

"Are you the woman who saw my daughter..." his voice trailed off.

"I am. I saw her pushed by the man lying in there."

Lucy's voice was small but firm. She reached over and put her hand on Anderson's forearm.

"I am so sorry."

"We need to go in, senator," Moore said. "Will you follow me, please?"

Johns put up his hand to arrest their movements.

"I received a phone message from Piers Cousins," he said. "May I speak with you privately, DCI Moore?"

He had Moore's complete attention.

"Okay," she replied. "Please give me a moment, gentlemen."

They walked together down a long corridor. Once out of earshot, Johns told Moore of his message.

"Piers said his wife, Helen, called him requesting the police hurry to a cottage owned by an Arthur McMurray near Tomchrasky. Helen said Edwin Montfort has admitted to killing Mr. Redfern. I'm going up there, but I need your approval."

Moore squinted and pursed her mouth.

"It's true I allowed Sasha Pelletier, Helen Cousins, and Martha Littleword to attend their meeting today. I've been busy all afternoon dealing with," she cocked her head the waiting room's direction, "this matter. I wasn't aware they were with Edwin Montfort."

"It's your investigation, Verity. I respect your authority, but those two women are important to me personally. Will you give me two of your constables to go find them?"

She was quiet, her hands on her hips and one foot tapping the linoleum floor. After a few moments of silence, she took a deep breath and exhaled.

"Johns, all four of those people are suspects in a murder investigation regardless of what Helen Cousins says about Edwin Montfort being the murderer. You know I'm not letting you go up there without me. Besides, it's not your jurisdiction and my superintendent will crucify me if I don't follow protocol. You'll wait until I have Anderson's identification of Redfern and then we will go together."

"Five minutes, that's all I'll wait," Johns said.

"You'll wait until I'm done, or I'll have you arrested for interfering with an investigation."

They both stood their ground, but a twinge of conscience pricked Moore's ego. After all, she owed him one. He'd given her the murderer of Coraliss Redfern. It was time to let bygones be bygones, if not friends.

"Merriam, I tell you what. Let me wrap this up, and I'll contact Glasgow to get us a fast ride with a big spotlight."

"Glasgow?" Johns echoed, looking confused.

Verity offered Johns a conciliatory smile.

"Yeah, that's where Scotland Police's Air Support Unit is based."

"A helicopter?" Johns asked, his face spreading into an enormous grin.

"Yeah, a helicopter," she confirmed.

She gave him a friendly pat on the shoulder and went to collect Senator Anderson.

Chapter Forty-Six

"We'll need his password," Helen said as the three of them huddled over Mufidy's cell phone.

The flashlight's upward beam cast a ghoulish glow upon their down-turned faces as they studied the phone's mechanisms. They'd tried multiple series of four numbers with no success.

"This is useless. We need another plan," Helen announced with annoyance. "Any ideas?"

"What if we go around Arthur's house and slip into the van, wake up Mufidy and he uses the phone to call for help?" Martha suggested.

"I used Arthur's phone when I went to the bathroom and called Piers. I told him to contact the police and get them up here."

"The problem is, where is here?" Martha pointed out. "We barely found this place. It's not on any maps. We can't go back into the house. Edwin is waiting in there."

"The only thing we can do, ladies," Sir Alec interjected, "is for you to slip around the house and get to the van. Edwin will come looking for Arthur and when he does, I'll do my best to slow him down."

"No!" Helen breathed. "I can't let you, Alec. I couldn't live with myself if you...if he..."

"Hush, my dear," Sir Alec said. "I may be in my seventies, but my youth taught me how to swing a cricket bat. That piece of lumber over there against the wall should work fine. Go to the van, wake up this Mufidy person, and call the police."

Helen and Martha exchanged quick, worried looks.

"I'll stay," Martha said. "You and Alec go to the van."

"NO!" Alec said with force. "Now go! The quicker the better and don't take the obvious route. I'll handle Edwin when and if he shows."

Taking them by the shoulders, he gently nudged them toward the low doorway.

"We don't have much time. You'll have to go by moonlight. If Edwin sees the flashlight beam heading toward the van, he'll know something is wrong."

Squeezing back through the tight tunnel, Helen was the first to emerge from the cell's aperture, but feeling a slight tug on her jacket, she stopped. At her ear, she heard Martha whisper, "He might be waiting outside. Stay close to the wall and in the shadows. Look and listen before you go."

The breeze coming from the outside was cool, sweet, and subdued. A luscious moon hovered in a cloudless night sky, spreading her almost pinkish glow with beneficent tenderness over her Earthbound subjects. With regal serenity, she reigned supreme over the night and need not worry herself, for there would be no usurpers powerful enough to rob her of her glory. She beckoned Helen to come free of the underground grave, promising her safe passage if she'd but trust in her wisdom and grace.

Soon a cloud pushed toward the moon like an ardent suitor, hastily, aggressively, and without her consent. A chilly wind blew up from nowhere, cooling the cloud's advances, but as Helen watched, the night's undisputed queen relented and accepted the cloud's favor, allowing him to cover her like a lover, if for only a moment.

Helen leaned free from the tunnel and seeing no one, slipped along the banked wall of the dug-out area followed closely by Martha. Nothing stirred, not an adder hunting among the grasses or a pine marten stalking his dinner. Only the hushing sound of wind through the trees let them know the landscape was more than an illusion.

Choosing to go up the opposite embankment from which they'd originally come down, Helen and Martha, after walking some five hundred yards in a wide arc, could see McMurray's house below them. The interior lights were off except for the one still alit in the lounge.

"Let's go down over there," Martha pointed at a sloping hillside to the left of the house. "It will take us down to the van and out of sight of the window."

With Martha in the lead, they picked their way slowly until they saw the van.

"I haven't seen Edwin move around inside the house," Helen whispered to Martha. "Do you think he's gone to find Arthur?"

The sound of metal scraping upon metal like a rusty hinge in need of oil indicated someone was on the move. Crouching, the two friends watched a man's shadow move up the same path Arthur had forced them to take only thirty minutes before.

Helen took the lead.

"Hurry," she whispered to Martha.

Within seconds they were at the back of the van pulling on the doors. The interior light came on overhead revealing Mufidy fully conscious but ready to put up a fight even though gagged and bound. He slowed his squirming at the sight of them.

"Calm your horses," Martha said, pulling the gag from his mouth. "We're the good guys."

"What is going on?" he yelled.

"Get quiet," Helen came back. "Edwin is a lunatic with a loaded gun, literally. He banged you over the head, tried to bury Martha and me alive, and admitted to killing Reny Redfern. We've got to call for help. You're the only one with a cell phone."

Martha was still working on the ropes securing Mufidy's legs despite his frustrated jerking, both physical and verbal.

"You're insane!" he cried, his voice carrying out into the night. "Was it you who took my mobile? If it was, lady, I want it back right now!"

Before undoing the last knot in the rope to release his legs, Martha got down in his face.

"Oh, stop your drama king crap. I've got your mobile," she said. "I took it from your pocket to save it from being confiscated by Edwin and being tossed down in some ravine where the rest of ours went. The story behind why we're all in this mess is too long to explain right now, Mufidy, but the short story ends with us dead in a ditch if you don't keep your cool and help us stop Edwin. Capisce?"

Like a tantrum-throwing three-year-old, Mufidy wriggled and writhed about as Helen and Martha watched with true female irritation and confusion at his inability to apprehend the severity of the situation. A gunshot brought his antics to a complete stop.

"Alec!" Helen breathed.

"Get my wrists free!" Mufidy cried.

"What's your mobile phone's password?" Helen demanded.

"I'm not telling you!" he yelled back.

Martha double-timed her efforts to release the tied-up man, and once free, he reached over, shut the van door, and climbed to the front where he sat down in the driver's seat.

"What is wrong with you?" Helen cried. "Sir Alec Barstow is up there with that maniac. We have to help him."

"Give me my phone," Mufidy growled. "You two can do whatever you want. Get out, club more people over the head, or jump off a cliff. I don't care. I'm leaving."

"You're not going anywhere," Martha said, sounding calm. "Besides, we don't have the keys. Edwin does."

"Yeah!" Helen joined in, supporting Martha's necessary lie. "We don't have the keys."

"You may not, but *I* do," Mufidy declared and popped open the glove compartment to reveal another set. "The guy who loans this van to us always keeps a spare. Give me my phone."

Martha and Helen looked at one another. They weren't leaving without Sir Alec. As tight friends, they always knew what the other was thinking. Martha pointed at Helen.

"Wanna go for three?"

Helen shrugged but picked up a heavy milk bottle resting in a crate.

"Two, this would make only *two*."

"Okay, okay, but three would have been a nice, lucky number for you."

"Shut up or get out!" Mufidy yelled and turning around to put the key into the ignition, he fired up the engine.

"What the heck," Martha said. "It is my turn."

Taking the milk bottle from Helen, she studied where Edwin's bump showed clearly on the left side of Mufidy's cranium. With a firm shot to the right side of his head, she sent him once again to dangle like a loose rag upon the steering wheel.

"Should we tie him up?" Helen asked.

"Nah, let's take this other set of keys, too. We still have the same problem. We're no closer to knowing the phone's password."

"Screw it," Helen said. "We've got to take Edwin out of commission. If he has so much as laid one finger on Alec, they really *will have* me on murder charges."

Martha nodded in firm agreement.

"I got it. Let's honk the horn and flash the lights. Edwin will come running. When he does, he'll only find Lumpy here," she pointed at Mufidy, "passed out. As Edwin is coming this way, we'll get inside McMurray's house, lock it up, and use the landline to call. We can stay on the phone with the police until they find this place."

"Let's do it," Helen said, reaching over Mufidy to check if he was still alive. "He's fine."

"Hit the horn," Martha said, "and get ready to run."

Helen nodded.

"On the count of three, One, Two, Three!"

The old grocery van came alive with barking horn sounds and flashing headlamps, plenty of noise to wake the dead, and hopefully detour Edwin.

"Let's go," Helen said heading out the back door.

"I'm right behind ya, sista. Go! Go! Go!"

Chapter Forty-Seven

"I'm here!" Johns yelled into his mobile phone. "We should have Helen and Martha's phones triangulated soon."

The sound of the EC145 police helicopter's blades beating the air made it nearly impossible for Johns to hear Piers asking what he should do next.

"Try to come up to Fort Augustus. We're waiting on a Sergeant McBride to arrive. He was out looking for them when he picked up one woman from the group. Yes, yes, the woman's name was Sasha Pelletier. She's corroborated Helen's statement about Edwin Montfort. McBride says he knows the approximate location of the road going to McMurray's cottage. Hey! Looks like it's time to go! Meet us here, if you can!"

Johns watched DCI Moore talk with the helicopter pilot as he ended his conversation with Piers. Ten minutes earlier, they'd dropped Lucy, Senator Anderson, and Special Agent Quinn at a decent hotel. Seeing the personal items of Reny Redfern would have to wait until the morning. Moore had more important fires to put out.

From the minute Piers told him of Helen's distress call, an all-consuming drive to get to Martha took hold of him, but he knew she might not be happy to see him either. This time he'd be less of a white knight charging in to save the day and more of a supportive friend. The last thing Martha would want is him crowding her, especially after what happened at the pub.

The helicopter, ready to go, sat in the middle of an empty parking lot. A bevy of police was attempting to keep the curious onlookers and a handful of stray dogs to the parking lots' perimeter. Both humans and canines appeared to be enjoying the exciting experience of a helicopter landing in the middle of the village.

A car arrived. Johns saw a woman and a police sergeant, who he took to be the long-awaited Sergeant McBride, make their way over to DCI Moore. A conversation ensued, and Moore waved Johns over.

"This is where my sergeant picked up Miss Pelletier. Along the road, there are a few old crofts tucked back along barely passable sheep trails."

Verity, holding a computer tablet, pointed to places on a satellite map for him to see.

"Miss Pelletier did not travel the entire way to McMurray's cottage, but jumped from the grocer's van and walked to the main road. If we ping the different phones, we find Helen Cousins', Martha Littleword's, and Sasha Pelletier's phones all in one place back here, whereas Montfort's and Mufidy's show up next to a cottage. I say we look in this area first."

"I agree," Johns added.

Verity nodded.

"Let's go. I've already sent a ground team toward this location. They should arrive within twenty minutes."

Seconds later, they were in the helicopter and getting ready to lift off. It was Johns' first helicopter ride, and it thrilled him. Given the seat next to the pilot, he looked down at the parking lot, watching the wind from the helicopter's blades whipping people's hair and clothes.

He zeroed in on a boy of about seven and his mother standing with other bystanders. The boy, his face transfixed with awe, seemed to mirror Johns' inner excitement. He gave Johns a thumbs up which Johns returned, bringing an enormous grin to the child's face. The helicopter lifted, hovered for a few moments, moved backward according to normal safety protocol, and took off.

Earlier, the pilot had handed Johns a pair of night-vision goggles. He put them on bringing the nighttime landscape into clear relief.

Adrenaline surged through Johns' being as the helicopter glided over the village, up into the higher elevations and westward into the Highlands.

⚅⚅⚅

THEY MADE THE TOP OF THE HILL TO THE EAST SIDE OF THE cottage when the sound of footfalls coming up from the pit's embankment arrested any further movements on Martha and Helen's part. Crouching behind a corner of the house, they had a perfect view of the van with its still illuminated headlamps below them.

With one hand, Martha crossed her fingers hoping Edwin would take the bait, and with her other, she unconsciously gripped the two sets of van keys down in her jacket pocket. Her mind registered an oddity. One set of keys had a fob attached to it.

Taking the keys out, she carefully inspected the set with the fob. In the moonlight, she saw a red emergency button on it. Would it work? What if it belonged to another vehicle owned by the greengrocer? Goodness knows the old van didn't look like the owners had equipped it with a modern electronic system.

A silent nudge from Helen shifted her thoughts from the keys. Someone was coming. Martha tried to focus her eyes in the dark to see. If the person was wearing glasses, it was their target, Edwin. If not, and the person was wearing a jaunty hat, it meant Sir Alec had bagged himself an Edwin.

Martha watched and waited, hoping she'd see Sir Alec's Fedora rise from the ground like a welcome specter bringing news from the underworld.

"Come on! Let it be Alec," she practically prayed out loud.

As if in answer to her command, a man's figure achieved the top of the hill. Where his eyes were, a glint reflected as the moon broke free from her cloud's embrace.

"No hat," Martha breathed, her shoulders slumping with disappointment.

"It's Edwin," Helen whispered down to her. "The gunshot we heard. We've got to check on Alec."

Edwin didn't move but appeared to consider the quiet van below him, its lights burning bright. Turning his head in a full sweep of the area, Martha watched as he studied his surroundings like a coyote or other predatory animal whose instincts told him something smelled wrong.

Feeling the fob again, Martha thought it was worth a try. If it succeeded, it would bring Edwin away from the one point of entry for the cottage. She pushed the button, resulting in only a barely audible 'humph' sound. Twisting herself around, she leaned closer and squeezed the button tighter, thinking perhaps the battery was low.

Like a half-drunk donkey being prodded, the horn cranked into life. With another firm push of the button, the lethargic, sad braying took off. The horn, losing its sluggishness and growing into a wild howl was accompanied by the van door swinging open and Mufidy being ejected onto the ground.

"Ooh," Martha said under her breath. "That had to hurt. What did I do? Was that some kind of anti-theft-catapult system?"

She heard Helen stifle a chuckle behind her, but say, "If it is, it's the best one I've ever seen. Hit the emergency button and anyone driving gets tossed to the curb."

Mufidy lay like a discarded bundle of laundry.

"Come on," Helen said. "Edwin's going down."

The distraction worked and as they darted to the back door, Martha caught the sight of Mufidy rolling around and raising himself to a sitting position.

With Helen hitting the entry door first, they were within

seconds locked inside the cottage. Martha pushed a heavy bureau in front of the windowless door to add a weighted barrier. If anyone tried to push it open, they'd have to work for a while.

Turning around, she saw Helen head for the bathroom.

"You went thirty minutes ago!" she called after her.

"I stuffed the phone in the towel bin!"

Not sure whether to stay put and fend off Edwin, or follow Helen, Martha decided to search around the entry hall for something to defend her position.

"I've got it!" Helen called, coming back from the bathroom. "I'm dialing 999."

"I'll keep watch on what's going on down below."

Getting down on all fours, Martha crawled over to the bay window and peeked over the sill to see Edwin shouting at Mufidy.

"What are they doing?" Helen asked as she dialed.

"They're busy explaining things to one another."

Pulling her head back, she rolled over and sat down on her bottom to survey the room as Helen got hold of the police. Sitting by the table was an expensive-looking briefcase.

"Ahh, what do we have here? I don't remember seeing you before."

In a few nimble movements, Martha crawled toward the briefcase and, unhooking the buckles, she looked inside.

"Helen!" she cried. "I think I've found them. Come here."

"What?" Helen said, appearing in the doorway. "What have you found?"

"I bet it's the originals. The copies are still on the table."

Helen's shoulders dropped a good three inches, and so did her jaw.

"Holy crap!"

Martha smiled up at her friend, rolled back down on her bottom, and laughed.

"Why, Lady Cousins, I don't think I've ever heard you use that word."

Like a woman transfixed, Helen started into the room.

"Wait! Get down," Martha directed. "We don't want them to know we're in here. They can see you if you don't crawl."

Nodding, Helen assumed all fours and met Martha half-way.

"Let me see," she said, her words sounding like a child who's about to steal a glance inside Santa Claus' gift bag.

Martha handed her the opened briefcase. With tender care, Helen pulled a linen-wrapped bundle from it and lay it in her lap. Like a mother cradling a fragile newborn child, she gently removed the protective fabric coverings to reveal the lost sections of the ancient Book of Kells.

"Holy smoke," Helen breathed.

Outside, a man's yell shut down the wonder moment.

"Did you hear that?" Martha whispered. "Wrap up the book and put it back."

Helen nodded. With a hurried but precise attentiveness, she re-wrapped the manuscript and put it in the briefcase.

"If we go out through the bathroom window, they won't see us. We should be able to get up to the top of the mountain. The police are on their way," Helen said, already in a duck walk out of the room.

"Through the bathroom window?" Martha said, her eyebrows elevated as she gave her butt a few pats. "Will I fit?"

"I'll let you go first, and I'll give you a good shove if I have to," Helen said turning around with a devilish grin.

"You're such a skinny butt," Martha said hoisting herself up again on all fours and crawling toward the hallway. "What if I get stuck in that tiny, European bathroom window? I could be murdered because I shoveled too many of those shortbread cookies in my mouth last night and this morning. This should be a reminder to me the next time I'm having trouble resisting food."

"Don't forget you also finished that bag of chips on the way up here," Helen teased.

"Better hope I squeeze through, Helen, because if I don't, we're both..."

A loud banging on the door with the bureau froze their progression.

"Crap!" Martha croaked. "Get up and get to the bathroom."

Edwin and Mufidy's voices, muffled but yelling, called for them to open the door. With Martha in the lead and Helen pulling up the rear, they made for the bathroom and frantically locked the door.

"That's it," Helen said, pointing at the window.

Sizing it up, Martha scowled.

"Should I go feet first? I don't want to drop on my head."

"Martha! Come on, we need to hurry!"

Climbing up on the toilet, she opened the window and poked her head outside. All clear. With a grunt, Martha hoisted herself up on the sill and wiggled her upper half through the opening without a problem, but as her ample hips hit the window frame, she came to a dead stop.

"Go on," Helen hissed.

"It's a smidge tight..."

Feeling Helen's always cold hands grab her ankles, Martha squeaked, "No, no, no!"

But it was too late, lifted into the position of an upended seesaw, Martha pointed nose-down toward the ground. Sliding through the window, she realized happily a sudden truth.

"I fit and that window was so little. I bet all the stress and hiking burned up the shortbread and few extra tiny indiscretions as well."

Scrambling back to her feet, she got up to help Helen. The briefcase came out, followed by Helen's upper body. Within seconds of getting her friend free of the window, they heard the bureau banging against the hallway's wall and the two men clamoring through the house.

"Up to the top of the hill," Helen said in a low tone. "The police should be here any minute soon."

In less time than it usually took Martha to order a Mocha

Frappe, she made the upper, most point of the hill behind McMurray's cottage with Helen coming up behind her.

"What's that sound?" Martha asked out loud. "I sure hope it's the calvary."

As she looked up into the nighttime heavens, a huge helicopter whooshed up from the other side of the hill and banked once, hovering like a great, black dragon right above them.

"Holy Batcopter, Helen!" she yelled, staring up into the metal underbelly of their winged savior. "It's not the calvary..."

⚜

"It's Martha!"

Johns grabbed the sides of his night-vision goggles.

"I'd know that wild mane of hair anywhere!"

The pilot maneuvered the helicopter, flying it in a sweeping circle of the area.

"We have a visual. Two female subjects on the ground," the pilot's voice said. "One appears to be waving and jumping. The other is carrying a satchel, ma'am."

A delighted smile broke out across Johns' face.

"Light up the ground," DCI Moore's directed.

With a flip of a switch on the pilot's dashboard, a bright column of light cut through the darkness, making slow sweeps until it landed upon Martha and Helen.

"I have two police units within ten clicks, ma'am," the pilot stated, meaning Moore's back-up officers still had ten kilometers to traverse with most of the terrain being rough and difficult. "We have another visual on two male subjects exiting the structure. Wait on confirmation of one male who may be armed. The two males are heading southwest in direction of the two females."

Johns, with his night vision glasses, saw the two men coming up the hill behind Helen and Martha. Within five minutes, they'd be upon them.

"We have visual confirmation, ma'am, a male subject wearing

glasses is armed," the operator monitoring the helicopter's infrared camera feedback said through the radio.

As he watched, Johns watched both women continue to wave. The sound of the helicopter made it impossible for Helen and Martha to hear the men's approach.

"Maintain our position and focus the light on the men," he heard Moore say to the pilot. "Give me an outside line."

"Copy," the pilot replied. "You have audio."

Moore's voice blasted out over the landscape.

"This is DCI Moore of the Fort Augustus Police. Please lay down your firearm. Please return to the house. Our officers…"

Johns was barely aware of the rest of Moore's statement, for as he watched, one man stopped. The other, holding a gun, continued to climb the hill. Helen and Martha started scrambling down the rocky hill in the opposite direction.

"We've got to get down there," Johns said into his microphone. "That side of the hill appears to be unstable."

As if his words had cast a spell, rocks started rolling down the steep incline below Martha.

"Stay put," Moore's voice boomed again, "officers are on their way. Do not proceed."

But it was too late. The man had achieved the hilltop where only seconds ago, Martha and Helen had stood. Going to the edge, he looked down. Both women were scooting on their butts away from him. They'd made it a third of the way, but unbeknownst to them, the hillside dropped off into a sheer chasm. If a landslide took hold, they'd be carried off the edge and to their deaths.

"It's going to cause a landslide," Johns stated firmly into his microphone. "We need to drop them a safety ladder."

Turning around in his seat, he looked Verity in the face. It was her call, but it needed to be now.

She nodded.

"Lower the ladder. Get above them."

The pilot maneuvered the helicopter into position. Sliding her door back, Moore dropped the ladder as Johns watched it come within two feet of Helen's arm reach.

"Give me the audio," Johns demanded.

"Give it to him," he heard Moore say in his ear.

With a nod of the pilot's head, Johns spoke.

"Martha, Helen, you've got to take hold of the ladder. Carefully stand up and grab hold. Drop the bag, Helen."

With the searchlight blazing down upon them, Johns easily saw the look of fierce refusal on Helen's face. She shook her head 'no'. Pointing down at the briefcase, she pointed back up at the helicopter.

"Leave it, Helen," he said. "Grab the ladder. Martha, stand up and grab the ladder, now! You can't wait. The ground below you is likely to give way."

He focused down on Martha's upturned face. With every fiber of his being, he wanted to reach down like the hand of God and save her. But with a gritty grin, she turned over and crawled back toward the top.

The ladder lowered perfectly within reach of Helen. Dumbfounded, Johns watched her pull the belt from her jacket, slip it through the briefcase's handle and tie it to one of the ladder's ropes. Holding on to the ladder and putting her foot on one rung, Helen bent down and reached out for Martha's hand. Within seconds, their hands locked, and Helen pulled her up until Martha grabbed the ladder. As Martha stepped onto the rung with Helen, the ground beneath them gave way.

"They're on!" he called. "Take it up."

The helicopter lifted and banked to the left away from the crumbling hillside. Clinging together on the ladder, Helen and Martha and one of the most precious books in all of Christendom, if not the world, took a winged flight out across a spectacular mountain landscape with the moon smiling proudly upon them.

Chapter Forty-Eight

In less than a minute, Martha and Helen crossed low hills, deep ravines, and a wide-open area over the main road. The helicopter lowered them within six inches of a level piece of ground where a police vehicle, its blue lights flashing, waited as a beacon for their landing. Shaken but safe, they stepped off their safety ladder into the secure hands of two helpful constables.

"We're okay!" Helen yelled above the helicopter's noise as it lifted off into the air once again. "Our friend is still there. He may be hurt. We need to go back to the cottage and show you where to find him."

The constable nodded and ushered them to the utility vehicle. Once seated, they explained about Sir Alec. The constable radioed DCI Moore with a search request and her response was quick.

"We have officers and a canine unit on the ground in pursuit of an armed subject. Forward location of a possible injured person."

"Ten minutes northwest of the house there'll be an archaeological site," the constable stated.

Minutes later, the radio came to life with good news.

"We have the individual in question. No injuries. Return to Fort Augustus Constabulary. Retain all parties until further instructions."

"Thank goodness," Helen sighed and leaned back into the padded seat. Great exhaustion poured over her. She shut her eyes.

Martha, her hair like a wild banshee's, leaned close and whispered, "You did it, Helen. You saved the book."

"We did it," Helen corrected. "What made you even look inside the briefcase? I would have ignored it."

Martha sat back in her seat and shrugged.

"Earlier, as we waited for you to come back and do your assessment, I couldn't help look around the room. Mostly, Arthur's taste ran to the monkish. Surprise. Utterly empty of anything comfortable or visually pleasing. Not one item or piece of furniture looked newer than 1970. So, when I saw the expensive hand-tooled leather briefcase sitting on the floor, I knew it wasn't there before. It had to be concealing something important."

Reaching down, Helen pulled the briefcase unto her lap. Gingerly, she pulled the manuscript out and unwrapped it. They sat quietly in admiration of the ancient text.

"It makes me sick to think Edwin would have sold it to someone outside of this country. This belongs to Scotland and its people. It's an icon of Scottish history and culture. It would be like selling off Westminster Abbey to the highest bidder and having it end up in some amusement park."

A gleam took shape in Martha's eyes as she resettled herself comfortably in her seat.

"Well, you're a gusty gal, Helen, and when Merriam told you to drop it, you put the book's welfare first. They will interview us and I plan on telling them what you did."

"Don't you dare."

"I most certainly will."

"Martha," Helen said, her tone like a hardened high school librarian who's about to hand out week-long detention to rowdy noise makers, "So HELP ME, if you even think about talking to the press, I will ...I will..."

"Oh, sit back and relax. I promise to be a paragon of cool."

"No, you promise me right now you won't talk to the press

about this," Helen demanded. "I've been implicated in a murder and forced to whop two men over the head in the last twenty-four hours. We will lose all credibility as a firm and probably be sued."

"Okay! Okay!" Martha cried. "I promise. But don't blame me when the press wants to know the backstory of how a lost section of The Book of Kells magically materializes from the dustbin of history."

Mollified, because she heard the surrender in Martha's voice, Helen settled back into her seat. The nighttime Highland's landscape slipped by noiselessly as both women stared fiercely out opposite windows.

Ahead of them lay Fort Augustus, a DCI full of hard questions, and one exceedingly angry mechanic who probably had a litigious looking bump on the right side of his head.

"Would you like to try some tea, dear? It soothes the troubles," the kind face asked bending down to her level.

Sasha sat in the police station's waiting room wrapped in a warm afghan hand-crocheted in Scotland's colors of blue and white. Around her shoulder, a sling hobbled her left arm. They'd given her some acetaminophen for the pain and sent Mrs. Fingle, a diminutive, round lady in her late sixties, who introduced herself as the constabulary's community volunteer, to nurse her. The sweet woman had tried at least three times to give Sasha tea, cocoa, or coffee, but each time she'd refused the offer. Maybe, Sasha thought, it would be best to give in to her ministrations.

"Do you have chamomile?" Sasha asked.

The concerned face lit up with a smile.

"We do! I'll bring it right over."

It was clear the town was low on crime. Mrs. Fingle even coerced the teenager brought in for trying to buy beer at the local supermarket to take a cup of hot cocoa. The youth sat sipping his warm chocolate and looking nervously at the door each time it opened. Sasha smiled to herself. They were both waiting for their mothers to arrive. His would probably drag him out by his ear. Hers had been relieved to hear she was okay.

Before Mrs. Fingle returned with the cup of comfort, Sasha heard the main door open, the bell tinkle to announce visitors, and two well-known voices arguing.

"It will be subject to DCI Moore's investigation," Helen said. "We will have to give it to the police."

"For how long?" Martha countered. "These places aren't that safe. Remember when someone broke into Marsden-Lacey's constabulary and stole the Brontë manuscript?"

"For the love of God! I don't know what will be..."

Helen came to a dead stop.

"Sasha?"

She hurried over followed by Martha, both taking up seats on either side of her.

"Look at you," Helen fussed, "honey, you've got a gash over your eye and your arm. Did you fall hard when you jumped from the van?"

Sasha wished the tea would show up. A sense of the horror from the last twenty-four hours was taking its toll.

"Yes, I rolled and wrenched my arm. It feels broken, but the police came not long after and brought me here."

Mrs. Fingle bustled over with the tea and thrilled to see two new bedraggled souls in need of cheering, she asked if they needed biscuits, tea, or a comforting blanket.

"I'd love all three," Martha said with enthusiasm. Forgetting her promise to leave off treats, she asked, "Do you have short-bread? They're my favorite."

"Of course, we do. I made some fresh today," Mrs. Fingle beamed, sharing Martha's hopeful smile. "I'll be right back."

All three seated women watched Mrs. Fingle disappear, most probably to a break room somewhere in the back. Sasha spoke first.

"I want to apologize for what has happened and tell you everything."

She took a deep breath.

"I went to talk to Reny in his cabin after dinner. He asked me to come and told me who he was. He wanted to know who I was working for. Earlier I refused to say who it was, but I thought it was safe somehow because he was my father. When I told him R&M Holdings, he smirked and asked what manuscript was I having appraised today. When I told him it was a Holinshed, he laughed and said apples don't fall from trees. That threw me, but then he asked about the Wytfliet atlas. He wanted to know if I knew who purchased it. I told him a blonde woman with curls bought it. I didn't know as I do now, the blonde woman was his wife."

"Wait!" Martha blurted. "R&M Holdings must have been Redfern and Montfort, not Reny Redfern but Coraliss Redfern."

"Do you think Reny knew what Coraliss and Edwin were up to?" Helen asked.

"I do," Sasha said firmly. "I believe after hearing Edwin's story, Reny thought I was working with them to manipulate him. He was smug and aggressive, threatening me and demanding to know what manuscript was being appraised today. If I didn't tell him, he said he would trump up some sort of charge against Emily and make sure she never captained another ship."

"Did you tell him?" Helen asked.

Sasha didn't hesitate.

"I did and once he knew, he laughed. His reaction was hostile like I'd deliberately hurt him. He said it was a criminal offense to sell something of such intrinsic cultural value and if I didn't make sure *he* got it instead of R&M Holdings, he'd make sure I went to jail."

"Oh Sasha," Helen said. "Why did you ever agree to broker a deal for something so valuable like The Book of Kells? You knew the law."

She nodded.

"I didn't know it was The Book of Kells missing section. I'd have *never* involved myself, Sir Alec, or you in something criminal. Two days before coming up to Banavie, I spoke with Mr. McMurray to confirm our appointment. He was so excited about our visit and he said it wouldn't be a Holingshed, but something much rarer. When I said this was extremely unusual and told him I'd selected experts based on the Holingshed, he told me not to worry. Anyone worth their salt in the field of ancient manuscripts should be able to give an opinion, he said. I told him I wasn't coming up unless I knew what we would be seeing. He told me he'd found the lost section of The Book of Kells. I laughed like he was telling a joke. That's when he told me about the dig behind his house and that he'd been copying the pages for fifteen years. Honestly, I think he slipped and told me. Afterward, he probably called Edwin and told him about his mistake."

Martha pointed to the briefcase at Helen's feet, "McMurray was telling the truth."

"Is it in there?" Sasha asked in awe.

"Yep," Martha answered, "and it was Helen who saved it from being lost forever under a mountain of rocks."

Sasha's eyes grew round, and she gushed, "Really? What happened?"

Helen brushed off Sasha's question with one of her own.

"So, when did you realize who Edwin was?"

"He introduced himself as McMurray's legal advisor before dinner last night and I asked him if we'd be examining a possible lost section of The Book of Kells. He said it may be, but absolute secrecy must be maintained. The experts must know nothing about what they would be seeing. When I explained something this culturally significant could not leave Scotland and I'd been advising a client based on McMurray's wish to sell, Edwin said there was no need to worry over something that wasn't even a sure thing."

"That fits," Helen said, accepting the hot mug of tea from Mrs. Fingle and thanking her. Shaking her head back and forth, she added, "Edwin wasn't going to tell you he was the 'M' in R&M Holdings, because if he did, you would have known something wasn't right."

Between nibbling on a cookie, Martha weighed in.

"He and Coraliss were using you. She let Reny know who you were, and she must have also asked for a divorce and hush money when she realized what her father and Reny were doing with the navigational software business. When Reny said she'd keep her mouth shut and leave without a dime, Coraliss found another way to get his money."

"This morning Reny came into my cabin," Helen said looking into her cup. "He offered me an insane amount of money if I'd bring him the manuscript. It shocked me, and I asked him to leave. He didn't, and I lashed out at him, but I never killed him."

Sasha sighed.

"No, Helen, neither you nor even Edwin killed my father."

Martha and Helen turned in tandem to look Sasha in the face. In a soft tone, Martha asked, "Sasha, do you know who killed Reny?"

"It was me. I killed my own father."

Chapter Forty-Nine

The statement hung in the air.

"I've already told the constable who drove me here."

Sasha raised the afghan and revealed the handcuffs anchoring one of her wrists to the bench's metal arm rail.

"He thinks I'm in shock, and I guess I am, but it was me who took Matteo's keys and stole the windlass after my conversation with Reny. I was afraid of him especially after talking with Emily. I wanted something to carry, and I'd seen the crew working the locks of the canal. The windlass was perfect, and I easily hid it in my room or my satchel, and no one was the wiser."

"How did it happen, Sasha?" Helen said, her voice low and kind.

"I was coming down the hall this morning and heard Edwin arguing with Reny in your cabin. Edwin hit him and practically ran from the room. I slipped inside and saw Reny laying on the ground. I went over to him. He rolled over and saw me. I've never seen such a malignant expression on a person's face. He reached up and put his hands around my throat. I struggled and he flipped me over on my back."

Sasha, with her free hand, reached up and pulled the high

sweater collar away from her neck, revealing great purple and blue bruises.

"Oh, Sasha," Martha whispered and put her hand down comfortingly on Sasha's arm. "You poor kid."

"I found the purse. It's amazing I could think at all. I got the windlass free and brought it down on his head. It took about four good hits, but he toppled off of me. I was scared and couldn't think straight, so I pulled and pushed him until I had him in the closet. I threw the windlass out the porthole window. I thought it would go into the canal. It didn't."

"Why didn't you tell the police?" Helen asked. "Sasha, they believe it's me or Piers."

"I'm sorry, Helen. I'm so sorry. The day we met at the pub I saw you taking notes. You're left-handed and I'm right. The police would have never had a case against you, and I told the detective that I'd seen Edwin coming from your cabin. I confessed tonight because I couldn't let the police think for one minute longer it was you or your husband. You've all been so good to me. It doesn't matter. I've admitted everything and I hope you'll forgive me."

"I do," Helen said, reaching around Sasha and giving her shoulders a light squeeze. "It's over."

"They won't put you away," Martha said.

"Martha!" Helen cried. "Why do you say it like that?"

"What? It's true," Martha came back. "It was self-defense. I don't know why you didn't just tell the truth…"

Martha stopped dead in the middle of her sentence.

"You didn't kill him, Sasha," she said. "You're protecting someone."

Sasha, looking rattled, shook her head vigorously.

"No, it was me. I killed my father. He…"

"Stop!" Martha commanded. "You didn't kill Reny. Who did?"

The main glass doors opened disgorging into the waiting room DCI Moore, Johns, three constables, Sir Alec, Edwin Montfort, and two police dogs. Right behind them came Piers, Emily Tangent, and Mufidy.

"Put Mr. Montfort in a holding cell," DCI Moore barked over the noise, "and I want statements from everyone."

Helen and Martha exchanged grim expressions, but upon seeing Johns, Martha got up and went over to him. He took her by the arm and led her over to a place out of the commotion.

"I'm so glad you're okay," he said looking down at her, the love in his eyes unmistakable.

"Thank you, Merriam, for saving us," Martha said. "You were wonderful."

"No," he said shaking his head. "I'm sorry I didn't trust you. I have something for you."

He kept his distance but reaching into his jacket he pulled out a little box of chocolates.

"I bought these for you in Edinburgh. They're heart-shaped. I know you love chocolate and these reminded me of you."

Martha's heart melted at the sweet gesture. He'd been probably carrying these around for days. Remembering her promise to The Big Guy Upstairs and feeling an upsurge of happiness, she reached up and put her arms around his neck.

"You old love bear. Thank you. I'm glad to see you, too."

Johns' mouth spread out into a smile. He pulled Martha up into his arms.

"You don't think I'm too fat, do you?" she asked. "I've been eating a lot of shortbread on this trip."

He laughed and squeezed her tighter.

"Are you kidding, me? You look and feel like you've lost weight."

Martha, delighted at learning she looked thinner, planted a kiss on the tip of Johns' nose, but there was one more thing she needed to know.

"Now," she said, still wrapped in his embrace, "I forgive you for trying to control my friend group, even if some may be male."

His eyes narrowed playfully as he beamed down at her upturned face.

"You know what?"

"What?" she asked, toying with his upper-most shirt button.

"You're a real pain in my..."

"Johns!" DCI Moore yelled, stopping him in mid-expletive. "Would you please lend a hand with the statements?"

He looked back down at Martha, who was smiling in her minx-like manner up at him.

"You better not have bopped anyone on the head, stolen anything valuable, or wielded a firearm against an animal, a human, or even an inanimate object," he warned. "They'll toss you in permanent anger management classes *after* you serve time in some detention center."

"Helen did most of the heavy lifting this time. I may have had to tap Mufidy once, just once, on his head, but he deserved it. He was being such a crybaby about being tied up and no help at all with stopping Edwin. But the real news, is I know who killed Reny Redfern."

Johns closed his eyes and Martha saw that one vein on his neck pop out. He let her slide back to the floor.

"You stay here," he groaned and looked up, scanning the room. "Helen! Piers! We better talk!"

Chapter Fifty

DCI Moore sat across the table from Martha Littleword. It had been an interminable day, but Moore knew the night would be longer. The Littleword woman had spent over an hour telling her about Montfort's involvement with McMurray, Pelletier being threatened to turn over a national treasure to Redfern, the van confession by Montfort based on a bag of potato chips, and why Helen Cousins, a left-hander, couldn't have killed anyone.

There'd even been a long, shockingly detailed story about the time Cousins, her left wrist with a sprain and lacking dexterity with her right hand, needed help from Littleword to get free from a tight body-shaping undergarment. If this represented proof of Cousin's inability to kill someone, Moore doubted Cousins would want the story to be made public knowledge in a court of law.

She'd seen Johns scoop Littleword up and embrace her. They were a couple; it was obvious, but after hearing Littleword's statement, Moore no longer harbored any residual animosity toward her old professional rival. Merriam Johns had his hands full, and she wished him well. In fact, she prayed for his survival. Best to try another tactic with the Littleword woman.

"So, we have a confession from Sasha Pelletier stating she killed her father," Moore said. "But you believe it was someone else. Who, Mrs. Littleword, do you think killed Reny Redfern? Quit beating around the bush. So far, we only have yours and Helen Cousins' word for it that Edwin Montfort confessed to you about hitting Redfern in the Cousins' cabin."

"I told you, that's immaterial now. Keep up, detective," Martha said. "Edwin's crimes are many, but he didn't actually kill Reny, and neither did Helen. Let me ask you something, instead," Littleword said, leaning back in her chair and lowering her eyelids like some tough customer in an old American crime movie. "Have you announced Sasha's confession to the group out there?"

"No."

"You should."

A desire to gnash her teeth and scream welled up in Moore, but she quelled it.

"Why, why, why should I announce it?"

"Because if you do, the person will be forced to come forward. Everyone out there still thinks Reny's killer was either Helen, Edwin, maybe Matteo, or even Piers. Go ahead, break your police protocol, and make a statement. You're wasting your time, my time, and some lawyer's time otherwise. Helen Cousins may have scratched Redfern's face for being a pig and Mufidy can whine all night about being coshed on the head, which I believe Edwin did twice, but what you *need* is Reny's killer."

Martha crossed her arms over her chest.

"Oh, I forgot one thing. You'll love this," she added.

Moore wished for deliverance.

"What?"

"Edwin said Senator Anderson and Reny were in cahoots in some software fraud involving federal airline policies. He said Reny's wife knew about it, and she confronted Reny and her father. She wanted a divorce, but they both stymied her. Probably to keep her quiet so they could make billions."

Moore's mouth dropped. There it was...deliverance.

"Anderson is dirty! I knew it," she blurted, grinning at Martha.

"Coraliss Redfern's emails to her husband, to her father, and to Montfort would prove it."

Martha was on a roll. She nodded, leaned in closer to Moore, and kept going.

"When Coraliss found out about her husband's past crimes, she found Edwin and they concocted a plan. Reny figured out their game and wherever Coraliss is, she won't be seeing any money."

Moore couldn't help grimacing in the way people do when they know something tragic. Littleword caught the expression. She pulled back slowly and studied Moore. Seconds passed.

"Is Coraliss dead?" Martha asked.

Moore nodded, adding, "Yes, and her father will have to live with the part he played in her death. Fathers and daughters, mothers and daughters," Moore mused. "This investigation has been filled with them. I'm glad it's over."

"Not over yet," Martha said in a soft tone. "Please go out and announce to everyone you have a confession from Sasha. Please do so, inspector, and you'll have the last piece in your puzzle."

Chapter Fifty-One

The crowd in the waiting room had been somber, grumpy, and tired of drinking tea. It wasn't typical for the police station to see so much action. Fortunately, someone, probably Mrs. Fingle, had the foresight to ask if everyone would like some takeaway from one of the local pubs. The brilliant idea met with wallets being pulled out and money being piled into the dear lady's hands.

Soon, a teenager driving a scooter with a box strapped to the back came zooming up into the parking lot. Johns and Piers went outside to relieve the kid of the box and hand him the money plus a substantial tip.

"Thanks!" the boy said. "We've never done takeaway before, but this could be a real moneymaker."

Johns and Piers chuckled at his enthusiasm.

"Well, you saved the day. Tell your chef, we appreciate it."

With the smell of fresh fried fish and chips coming up through the paper sacks, the men hurried back to the waiting group. The first smiles in hours spread among the detainees. As they'd made their first tantalizing forays into the fish, DCI Moore and Martha returned from giving the statement.

"That smells wonderful!" Martha said. "Anybody want to share?"

Only hostile grunts answered her, but Helen motioned Martha to sit by her. Moore stayed quiet. Surveying the room, she saw the people were as tired as she was. It went against all her training, all her principles, and might get her in hot water, but it was worth a shot.

"Miss Pelletier has made a confession and admitted to killing Reny Redfern," she said to the group.

All eating stopped. Everyone turned and focused on Sasha, who swallowed the food in her mouth but didn't look up from her takeaway box.

"No, she didn't!" Emily Tangent declared.

Sasha reached out and grabbed her mother's arm. DCI Moore saw the pressure being applied by the grip.

"Emily," Sasha said, staring her mother down. "It was in self-defense. I had to. I've already given a statement."

"No, no, no," Emily repeated, an expression of wild worry on her face.

She put her takeaway box down on the table in front of her, turned toward her daughter, smiled, and put a hand over Sasha's.

"No, Sasha," she said gently, "*I* killed Reny and I don't regret it. He would not take you away from me again, ever again. I love you, my dear, sweet girl, more than life." Emily reached up, and with an encouraging smile for her child, she brushed the hair away from Sasha's face. "Everything will be okay. It will all be fine."

The room was silent. Some things are more holy than relics, more valuable than money, and more tenaciously protected than power. A parent's love, when it dovetails completely with selflessness, is a profound thing.

"Why did you kill Redfern, Ms. Tangent?" Moore asked.

Emily looked up at the inspector as if seeing her for the first time.

"He would have killed her. He was choking her. I had to stop him."

"You should have said something when I took your statement on the boat."

Emily shook her head.

"I can't explain it. This has all happened in less than twenty-four hours. I'd just found my daughter, and I didn't want to lose her."

Tears pooled in Emily's eyes, but she went on.

"Once I started hitting Reny, I hit him and hit him and hit him. All the rage and fear, what he'd tried to do to Sasha, poured out of me. I don't regret it, inspector. It was like shooting a rabid dog who has your child by the throat. You'd kill them and feel nothing but relief, complete and utter relief."

Chapter Fifty-Two

S ummer was ending, but its beauty was timeless. Everywhere butterflies, bees, and other winged creatures went about their daily duties in Healy House's garden. A crystal blue swimming pool lay like a postage stamp in the middle of a trimmed, green lawn bordered by rose bushes and tall hedges. Occasionally, the pool's water rippled as the breeze knelt and brushed it with a kiss. It was good to be home.

"Is this Heaven?" Martha murmured. "I'm so glad you married Piers."

"Glad you're glad," Helen mumbled back, her eyes shut and giving her polished pink toes a wiggle.

"I wish we had some lemonade to go with the potato chips. Salt and sour, a perfect pairing," Martha mused, deliberately repressing her promise to quit chips if God delivered her from Edwin's murderous grasp.

Like a jack-in-the-box, she popped straight up in her chair and slapped Helen's thigh.

"Hey! What was that for?" Helen yelled.

"That's us, Helen. We're salt and sour."

One of Helen's eyes opened to regard Martha but shut again.

"Who's the sourpuss?" she asked dryly. "*You?*"

Pulling the stashed bag of potato chips from under her lounge chair, Martha explained as she fed herself.

"You have to admit there's some truth in it."

Helen reached over and grabbed Martha's bag of chips from her grasp. For a few seconds, she munched on chips without answering.

"Maybe," she finally said, "but I think you and I are more like the two sides of a coin. We share a lot of the same good and bad traits. We're both sour *and* salty depending on our mood or the situation."

"Diplomatic as always," Martha conceded, yet eyeing the dwindling bag. "Are you done with my chips?"

A slow, mischievous grin spread across Helen's face as she hugged the bag tighter to her chest.

"Now, who's sour-acting?" she asked.

Martha chuckled.

"You win. I'll be sour if it'll get me my chips back."

With the bag retrieved and stashed again on the opposite side of her chair and out of reach of Helen's paws, Martha resumed her prone position in the lounge chair.

"I've been thinking about Sasha. How did the ceremony go?"

"Great! Donations from around the globe are pouring into Scotland's National Trust for the conservation of the newly found Book of Kells section. Sir Alec's team from Cambridge will assist with a portion of the work. All in all, it worked out well."

"I guess Edwin and Arthur will serve their time in Inverness."

Helen nodded.

"Yes, after the hospital releases Arthur. An adder bit him when he was in the cell. That was the gunshot we heard. Edwin killed it. Not a legal thing to do. They're a protected species in Scotland, so Edwin can tack on a few more months to his stay in prison."

"I knew those snakes were out there," Martha said, giving a shiver. "The entire time we were scrounging around in that underground cell, my skin was crawling. Poor old Arthur, he's had a tough run of it. I'm glad Emily's serving only one year and allowed probation. She and Sasha deserved better. What a mess one person can make in so many lives. Reny Redfern was a devil."

"Oh, you don't need to worry about Sasha," Helen said with a knowing smile. "She inherited Reny's entire estate, and she told me she plans to share it with her mother. Good things do happen to people. Which by the way, did you see Senator Anderson is facing a congressional hearing?"

"Good! I hope they lock him up and burn his navigational software. Safe flying, not profits, should be the priority. Makes a person terrified to get on a plane."

"Well, the police found Reny's and Coraliss' laptops in Piers' car trunk. There were all sorts of emails about Senator Anderson's involvement in manipulating the regulations on testing and implementing new navigational software into planes. He's a dirty boy if ever there was one."

They slipped again into a peaceful silence until out of nowhere, Helen asked, "Wanna go on a girl's trip to New York City? Piers wants to make up for ruining our girls'-week. He says he owes you one."

Martha sat bolt upright once again in her chair and looked at the reclining, sphinx-like Helen.

"REALLY?" she asked. "Just old salty me and sour you?"

With eyes still shut, Helen laughed. Making a hand gesture of a plane taking off, hitting turbulence, and nose-diving, she said, "You'd have to f-l-y-yeee."

Martha regarded her smug friend for a second. Reaching over quietly, she hovered her hand a good foot above Helen's still red thigh and smiled wickedly.

"Better pack your bags, you sour-sass, cause New York City here we ..."

Her hand hit Helen's thigh with a loud smack.

"...come!"

THANK YOU FOR READING!

Made in the USA
Monee, IL
17 April 2021

66075093R10138